Chapter 1

Sopl

CW01095146

Sophie Rush, a bubbly, beautiful and curvaceous 40 something, single mother of two girls, had spent the last six years as a single parent. Sophie really had to work hard to make it through life, but as hard as it was, she managed and quite successfully too. Sophie had worked her ass off within the marketing company she had worked for, for the last 20 years and as a result now held a senior position. Life wasn't perfect by any means, but she was happy with her lot. Most days she would hear the same speech from her children about meeting a man and settling down with someone, but she was never one to settle - certainly not for anything less than what she wanted. The one; she most definitely would never chase after a man. As she would say to her children Emily and Marie "An egg doesn't swim to the sperm, never chase a man!". That's not to say Sophie didn't miss companionship, having someone to cuddle with now and then and to feel loved and protected. Truth is her love life had been one disaster after another, a total train wreck. She always fell hard and fast but unfortunately found herself incredibly bored after the honeymoon period was over, and if that didn't happen the men would turn out to be controlling narcissistic freaks! Sophie was a magnet for these types of people, they would start out really promising, amazing sex, amazing personalities, then like the flick of a switch suddenly it would change, and she would end things. Sophie really felt at 40 years old this was her life – she was doomed when it came to love and was destined to be a spinster forever. She was lucky in every other aspect of life: she had amazing friends and family, enjoyed her job, and achieved a lot – she felt fulfilled in mostly every way possible. There was just this one thing missing: someone to share her life with, someone totally spontaneous, funny, and ambitious and so attractive she couldn't keep her hands off. She wanted a love that consumed her and she wanted that honeymoon period to last forever – not much to ask, right?

As she sat there in her own little world, as she often would, dreaming about the impossible, she looked up to the TV. "Wow!" Sophie was gobsmacked when she saw the hottest god damn man she'd ever laid her eyes on! He was none other than the up-and-coming actor Finn Holston. He was lovely and tall with blonde hair and blue eyes, just the right

amount of stubble on his perfectly imperfect face.
He had a body to absolutely die for and a smile that
could light up the whole world. She was sure he was
that charismatic he could get anyone to do what he
asked – he could be a frigging superhero, negotiate
peace with his charm and put an end to all that is bad
in the world. She'd never seen this man before or
even heard of him, yet she was bowled over from the
off. She went on to spend all night watching
anything and everything she could find on Finn,
from YouTube videos to fan-made Tik-Toks. The
popped up an advertisement: he was attending
Comicon in two weeks and was selling photo
opportunities and autographs for no less than the
extortionate price of £250!!!! As she lay there
watching in amazement, Sophie told herself that he
was The One and no one else could match him. She

told herself she had to meet this guy, by any means possible and hoped to god that if he saw her, he would want her as badly as she wanted him. She was well aware this sounded like she was an absolute psychopath but didn't care - she had to meet him!

Chapter 2

Pig man

Monday began with a bang – literally! "Fuck" - I was awoken abruptly and painfully as I fell off the bed, not knowing where the hell I was or what had happened. Once I'd managed to peel myself up off the floor and check I'd not put a hip out of place, I looked at my phone and realised it was Monday. I made my way to the shower looking like a zombie, walking like an OAP. Why was it after the age of thirty, literally everything aches when you get out of bed? As I entered the bathroom, I caught a glimpse of myself and sighed "And I wonder why I am single." I must've slept so heavily I had dribble up the left side of my face and my hair was everywhere!

As I turned the shower on, I prayed for it to heat up quickly; as I stood there freezing, my nipples were so hard I was worried they would cut into the mirror in front of me. Finally, after what felt like an eternity, I jumped in the shower. As the beads of warm water hit my skin, memories of the amazing dream I had began to consume my brain. Watching all those videos of that hot fucker all night must've made me dream of him. And as I reminisced, I pulled the shower head in between my legs and enjoyed every dirty thought I could get before my wonderful daughter banged hell out of the door, which brought me back to reality pretty quick!

'MAM, HURRY UP IN THERE!' Emily screamed at her me. "Fucks sake" I said under my breath, before yelling back "YES I KNOW, I'LL BE OUT IN 5, GIVE ME A BLOODY CHANCE." Time was precious in this bathroom since we only had one: it wasn't a rare occurrence for us to fight over the toilet, or for someone to come in and take a massive shit, whilst I was in the shower. I'm very glad I remembered to lock the door this morning.

Once I'd finished getting ready and had breakfast, I did the usual thing of screaming up the stairs for no less than twenty minutes for Emily and Marie to hurry up or we were going to be late. Honestly, expecting those kids to hurry up was like asking a turtle to fucking run; I had no hope in hell and I got worked up every god damn morning over it. I swear if they were ever ready on time I would die of shock.

"I'm on the highway to hell" I sang at the top of my lungs. Well sang is maybe not the right way to put it as my singing voice was fucking dreadful, but I was enjoying myself that was the main thing. As I pulled into the car park at work, I said to myself "Please no pig man, please no pig man, not today." With that I turned into my space and there he fucking was getting out of his car. "Oh, for fuck sake, happy fucking Monday Sophie, fuck my life." I always tried my best to avoid him because he literally made my skin crawl; I know that sounds nasty, but he really was as creepy as they come. But my luck being what it was, I always seemed to bloody run into him. "Wit woo" Nigel said as I got out of the car, he was literally standing by my door, waiting to pounce. I swear he'd fucking teleported across the car park, because from the time I turned my head to open my door, he had moved about 300 yards across the car park. He was out of breath so am guessing he ran, at that speed maybe he should be a fucking Olympian athlete, not work in finance. "You're looking especially hot today, let me take your bags for you." Here we go, why was it always me this had to happen to, why couldn't he stalk some other poor woman, there were plenty here, and every last one of them found my situation fucking hysterical. "Thanks, I had a wash! I'll get them, they contain top secret items, but thanks." Christ I shouldn't of said that, he licked his lips like he was about to eat me or something. I never gave him the impression I wanted him, sometimes I was really fucking brutal and he still came back for more, he wouldn't give up. Pig man had asked me out no fewer than 1000 times, he was bloody relentless! I just wish he would meet someone or get another job and move. He was one of those really greasy and slimy guys, that didn't seem to wash much and had white bits in the corner of his mouth. "My god just leave me alone" I muttered under my breath, as I practically ran up the stairs to my office; I was glad he worked on the first floor so he had no excuse to follow me all the way up.

Work was pretty much the same as always, absolute chaos – but that's how I liked it, too busy to think straight. Then came my 12pm meeting, "hope there's a fit guy coming in today" I winked at my colleague as I left the office and went into the meeting room. To my total astonishment there bloody was! He was tall, muscular, so muscular you could see it through his tight shirt, bright blue eyes and just all round sexy as fuck! This didn't happen often, but I loved it when it did. I was, like many women, a dirty bitch and had many fantasies; one of which was being fucked by a stranger in the office! And as I was sitting there listening very attentively to everything he said (yeah right), I started moving my legs slightly on the chair where I was sat, so I could feel my clit rubbing on the seam of my tights. After a few moments I was soaking wet and imagining him getting up, moving the desk out of the way, picking me up and throwing me on it as he kissed me and gently rubbed my wet pussy. What turned me on even more was the fact I was wet and playing with myself, looking this guy dead in the eye and no one had a clue what I was doing. Then I had to come back down to earth when we went around the table for any other business. I fucking have some, can tight shirt over there throw me over the desk and ravage me please? Then some twat asked me a question, what did they do that for? I had no fucking clue what this meeting was about, I'd spent the last thirty minutes in fucking dreamland, fucking moron. I had to come back down to earth pretty quickly, and form some kind of response, to be fair even I had an outer body experience, just look at myself and think what the fuck are you talking about. Usually, I was shit hot when it came to work, if I acted like that in every meeting, I wouldn't have a fucking job to fuck up in the first place.

After such an eventful and pleasurable day in work, I met up with some friends for a few cheeky drinks to unwind. Cara, Lisa, and Kelly were my three best friends – they very often met up for a few glasses of wine after work just to vent, talk crap and moan about men and life in general. All three were cringingly loved up with their boyfriends, and don't get me wrong I was happy for them, I just didn't want to hear about how wonderful their men were every two bloody minutes. What didn't help matters was that I just couldn't even find anyone decent to hold a conversation with, never mind a relationship. I wanted a knight in shining armour and all I ever got was a twat in tin foil.

"Show me the fucking Gin girls!" I fucking needed this today, big time. "Already ordered" Cara said as she passed me the ice-cold glass: what a woman. Cara was the nicest person you could ever meet; she would do anything for anyone and had a heart of gold, she did love getting involved in other people's business though, especially mine. Cara had always gotten screwed over by men, she like me had a colourful and unlucky love life, but recently she met the most incredible man and was hopelessly in love. "So how was everyone's day today?" I said looking over at them all. "Well, I've had an amazing day, I've been at the spa all day, Dale booked for us to go as a surprise." I loved Lisa to bits, but she always jumped from one relationship into another, so it was hard to take her seriously. Every man she met was 'the love of her life', and she admitted it, she was a relationship type of girl. "Oooh check you out, sounds lush. Mine was alright, not nice and relaxing like yours though. I saw the sexiest guy today in the office, wouldn't have said no to that! Other than that, nothing exciting happened."

"So, what did you do about it? Did you ask him for his number?" Kelly was very direct, she could never get it into her head that I was quite old fashioned in some ways and would never approach someone for their number, they always had to ask me first. She met David at a work's conference, and she was the one that approached him; she always says, "If you don't change the way you think, you will never meet anyone." Kelly, Cara and Lisa were all of the same opinion: that I was way too picky, but I don't think you can be too picky when it comes down to matters of the heart. "God no you crazy woman, I was in work, that would've been a bit unprofessional." As the words came out of my mouth, my subconscious told me I was a bloody hypocrite and said you didn't think masturbating was unprofessional when you were doing it earlier.

"Anyway" - I felt a swift change of subject was in order - "How's the wedding planning going Lisa?" It worked; Lisa's face just lit up like Blackpool in September! "Oh, it's going really well, hit a few snags, but nothing that couldn't be sorted, I just can't wait to marry him and have all eyes on me, you know I have had everything planned since I was 4. Just need to go dress shopping now, which I wanted to speak to you guys about. How are you all fixed for the first Saturday in March? I know it's a few months away yet, but I know how busy you all are, well apart from you Soph".

"Is that a nice way of saying I have no life Lisa?" Fuck's sake!!!! I thought by changing the subject I would give me a rest from the constant fucking reminder that I have no life and I'm totally undatable! All three of them gave me that look of pity; glad I came out tonight just to have this crap.

"Have you found a plus one to bring along yet Soph?" I was waiting for this; it was normally the first question she asked me. Lisa waited anxiously for my response, which by the way had been the same response she had for the last few months! "Just for the record yet again girls – I don't need to bring a man, I am quite capable of coming on my own, without a plus one. Besides there is only one man for me now and he is unobtainable as fuck. Unless I pay £250 to meet him in two weeks, he won't even know I exist!" All three of them raised their eyebrows. "Sophie what the fuck are you on about now, you're not hiring a male escort to come along are you? Cause that's just a whole new level of desperation." All three of them looked at me like I had finally reached a new low. "No, you bell end! Finn Holston, I saw him on TV and literally he is the most amazing man I've ever laid my eyes on. He's the one, I know he is, the £250 is for a ticket to go and meet him up in London at the Comicon." All three of them raised their eyebrows as if to say I needed to be committed as a matter of urgency. "You do know this is a ridiculous fantasy, right? Even if you spent the money to go meet him, he's famous, why would he want someone half normal? He's literally got the pick of the bunch. I love you Sophie, but this is stupid, how can you think he is the one when you've never even met him?" Cara ripped into me, here we fucking go, god I know friends are meant to be honest, but that's a bit fucking brutal. But at least she said I'm half normal.

"This needs to stop, you've finally lost the plot, get on a bloody dating app like we told you to and meet some normal people." That was the joke of the century, I'd been on these apps before, and I had never met anyone 'normal'. Then Cara got up excitedly and said "Oh my fucking god I have the best idea, let's make a deal. We will all chip in and get you a ticket if that's what you really want, provided you let us set up an account on tinder and pick out dates for you – a different one every night of the week. You have to go and meet these people though and give them a proper chance, keep an open mind and don't be shut off from the word 'go'." Christ could this sound sadder, as if I can't get my own dates, which by the way I am more than capable of, just don't like any of them. Is it really worth all this shit just to go meet this guy? What kind of morons are they going to be sending me on dates with? Fuck it, what did I have to lose, so through gritted teeth I muttered "Ok then deal, provided I pick what pictures you use." Cara's face said it all, she was so excited, she loved medelling in people's affairs. "Ok we get to write what we want in your bio though and you just make sure you're available tomorrow at 7pm for date no one."

I'm going to massively regret this, I know I am, as I nod and down the rest of my third gin in one.

Chapter 3

The disastrous love life of Sophie Rush.

As I got home, I stuck the TV on and sat there staring into space for a while, reminiscing about some of the disastrous dates I'd had. There were the usual, catfishes which was always fun and then there were my top two worst dates of all time.

First there had to be Mike, he was lovely looking, and we got on quite well. I proceeded to get absolutely wankered and we ended up in the back of his car, where things rapidly got out of hand. One-night stands were not my type of thing, I just didn't see the point; the sex always ended up being totally shit and I always went home feeling cheap. Anyway, I got carried away and started sucking him off, then he literally shot what felt like a tonne's worth of cum into my fucking tonsils. Now, I always liked to swallow, because as my mates would say, I was a fucking pig. But this was fucking ridiculous! As it hit my tonsils I heaved and retched and made the most awful sound as if I was being sick. Once I'd composed myself, with tears running down my face, I just said, "I'm ever so sorry." From there on in it was a rather awkward drive home. Needless to say, I never saw Mike again, nor would I want to, I was fucking mortified.

And then there was piss flap Pete. Telling these stories I sound like someone that always fucks on first dates, but I don't, honestly, these are the two of the rare times, and they happened years ago. Anyway, again alcohol was involved, and one thing led to another and I sat on his face. It started off lovely and then I don't know what fucking possessed him, but he got my piss flaps in his mouth and sucked and pulled them off. I remember shouting my fucking head off, it hurt so much that I wanted to bite his fucking bell end off. I got up, put my clothes on, gave him some pointers how not to lick someone out and then left, walking like John Wayne with the sorest piss flaps in the country.

Then there were the disastrous relationships I'd had. Firstly, there was Daniel, I truly loved him and spent a long time with him, we just grew apart and things turned sour fast, but I had some really good times and good memories with him. He was an absolute nightmare at times, but the sex was fucking phenomenal, really spontaneous, we would literally fuck anywhere and everywhere. If there was a chance of being caught, we would do it; was such a

.ull, I would look at him and want to rip his clothes off and he was the same with me: his hard cock was evidence enough for me without even having to touch him. Unfortunately, though, like most things it ended and bitterly. I wish we could've stayed friends, but he hated me so it would never happen. I do wonder sometimes if he was the one and I should've just persevered, but when I think back to how controlling and selfish, he could be, I did the right thing by leaving.

Then there was Jim the quim – Christ what a fucking bell end he turned out to be, and a massive one at that! It was amazing at first, like something from a fairy-tale: met him online, and when we met in person we had amazing chemistry. Not only that he was so kind, thoughtful and caring, he would help out with cooking and cleaning, bring me flowers and chocolates. Only thing missing in this relationship was good sex, but he more than made up for that with what he could do with his tongue…... phenomenal.

We moved in together after around six months of being in a relationship and things were great. He proposed and we got engaged, then boy did I see a change in him! Pretty much instantaneously he turned into a totally different person. He really was a nasty bastard, and a controlling one at that. That's one thing I hate - someone trying to control me; I am independent and can manage on my own, I don't need anyone, so the first sign of anyone trying to control me I begin to retract and rebel against the person. If I was meant to be controlled, I would've come with a remote control! Anyway, I fucked him off and bloody glad I did too!

Next was Fuck Face Frank, how the hell do I begin to describe him, he was my kryptonite, literally the only man to absolutely ruin me, emotionally and physically. You know the term an egg doesn't swim to the sperm, don't chase a man? I did not take any notice of this when it came to him, I literally was obsessed. He had a cock bigger than the Eiffel tower and being perfectly honest that fucking hurt me. Every woman I know always says 'god I want someone with a massive cock', no you fucking don't my love, not unless you want to have no fucking uterus left! Typical Libra would reel me in and talk to me constantly day in day out for weeks on end, we would see each other, have really deep and meaningful conversations, I really felt connected to him on a higher level than I'd had with anyone else. He'd show me he loved me in so many different ways, then he got bored of playing the game and messing with my emotions, so he'd rip my heart out, and stomp all over the fucker, and if that wasn't enough ghost me completely! What a fucking knob, god I hated him, and I hated myself more for believing the absolute bullshit that spouted from his mouth. But god when I think back to some of the messages, I sent him, fuck it makes me cringe. Me and Cara very often reminisced which made me feel physically sick. All I know is I hope to god I never see him again as long as I shall live, amen.

Last but not least was the total fucking whirlwind that was Caleb the cock. I actually have some really fond memories of him, even though it was a forbidden love, we had so much fun and genuinely I thought we would end up together, but as usual I ended up getting my heart broken. I'd known Caleb a very long time and always had a bit of a thing for him, there was just something about him, you know? No, with Caleb, there was literally nothing missing, perfect sex, best sex of my life, he was a dirty bastard, and I loved every minute of it. Conversation was brilliant, we were always laughing, chemistry was out of this world. We felt 100% comfortable around each other so much so, one morning we woke up he got up for a pee and my period pad was stuck to his leg. Words could not describe how I felt at that point in time: at first, I was absolutely mortified and had it been anyone else, I would've wanted to disappear up my own asshole. However, once he started laughing, I couldn't stop either. But unfortunately, that wasn't meant to be, and he fucked off back to his ex. Not going lie it broke me a little bit too in the process. To be honest after the pad incident I can't say I fucking blame him.

Fuck no wonder I am single, think I am just better off staying this way, no man to tell me what to do and no fucker to please or impress. If I wake up with a dislodged pad to the face it doesn't matter – only I will see it. Feeling a tad pissed now not going to lie, bedtime for me – I can finally fuck myself like I wanted to this morning, and I will sleep like the dead.

But before I do that, I'll see how the online dating is going. Let's give Cara a bell "Cara, just wondered if you'd had any messages on tinder?" Great, all I can hear is her absolutely pissing herself. Cara said "There's a few possible ones, but a few crazies too - will screenshot you one and send over now, I can't stop laughing."

"Oh, for fuck's sake! "I really am doomed, I'm going to bed now, will speak to you tomorrow for an update, Love you!" After Cara stopped laughing, she said "I love you too babes will catch up tomorrow with instructions for your first date!" Fucking date, I thought, what fucking date, this could actually work to my advantage.

If they don't find anyone tidy, they will A) leave me the hell alone and B) I get to go and meet Finn without having all of this drama on the lead up to it.

With that, my head hit the pillow and I was dead to the world.

Chapter 4

Shit luck, good luck

Tuesday started off quite nicely if I do say so myself; when I woke, I was in a really happy mood, feeling really positive and excited to meet Finn in the next few weeks. Fuck I hope to god I don't have to go on a date tonight with a complete knob. It would be good if I could get away with just going on the one date to shut the girls up and still get what I want, to meet Finn, rather than having to go on a date every day of the week, not to mention I do like to be in bed by 8 pm to have some me time and chill. Christ if I met someone, I would have to stay up past 8 pm and share my bed, I honestly don't know how I would cope not being able to starfish across my king size bed and enjoy every inch of it.

Time to get up, shower and short my hair and face out ready for another fun filled day in the office. "Oh my god! Marie, you've blocked the toilet again!!" This was a regular occurrence. Marie seemed to think that in order to wipe her arse effectively she had to use a whole fucking roll of toilet paper. "Marie, get in here and sort it out, you are eighteen years old, I'm done sticking my arm down the toilet to grip your shit." It actually smells like something crawled up her asshole and died, good job I don't have a weak stomach, or I'd be fucked. I love her to bits; she is my world but she drives hell into me especially when she blocks the only toilet in the house. Marie is moving away soon to go to university for three years, which is going to be hard, we've never been away from each other for more than a few days. One thing for sure as much as

I will miss her I won't miss these scenarios in the mornings.

That drama over, toilet unblocked, bladder emptied, showered and teeth brushed, time to get ready for work and sort my face out. "Ahhhhhhhhh" bloody mascara brush just scraped my eyeball off, god damn it, beauty really is pain! Can't wait to get pink eye and look like the elephant man on my potential date this evening. Every day I get closer to sticking a fork in a toaster! Think today is going to be one of those days. No it's not, think positive thoughts Sophie, think positive thoughts.

"Today's drive to work calls for a bit of Muse". 'As supermassive black hole' started blasting through the speakers of the car, I stopped at the traffic lights where the lady in the car next to me was less than impressed that I had this music on full volume at 7 am on a Tuesday morning. "You set my soul alight" I sang at the top of my lungs and smiled at her just to piss the woman off even more. She shook her head in disgust, the light changed to green, and I put the pedal to the metal and spun off laughing to myself. I'm not letting anyone, or anything ruin my bloody good mood today: I've been greeted with shit, been stabbed in the eyeball by my mascara brush and been judged and deemed a disgrace by a random woman, but nothing is going to get me down, not today! In a few weeks, I was going up to London to meet the man of my dreams - and at the moment that was what was keeping me going. Though I knew as time went on, I would be absolutely shitting my pants, and no doubt go mute at the sight of him.

"Yes! No pig man." Nigel was nowhere to be seen this morning, what a bloody relief; see, when you think positive, positive things happen. And pulling into the car park and pig man not being present was a very positive situation. Today is going to be a really productive day, and with any luck my wonderful friends hadn't found anyone for me to go on a date with tonight.

It was at that exact moment my Fit bit vibrated and there was a message from none other than Cara, 'be at the pub at exactly 7 pm you are on a date with John.' "Oh, for fucks sake!" I feel physically sick now. I hate meeting random people for dates, I either clam up because I fancy them and want to rip their clothes off, or I don't shut up and talk their heads off because I am nervous. Or of course there is the other alternative where I really don't fancy them, but they like me, it's a cruel trick of fate. What the hell am I going to wear? I wonder what he looks like, how will I know it's him? I can feel a panic attack coming on, I need to calm down rapidly. Just breathe Sophie, deep breaths, I know what I'll do, I'll ask Cara for a pic maybe that'll make me feel a little better, or if he's drop dead gorgeous will make me feel worse ahhhhh. Well Cara was very accommodating and told me no, which means I am going in completely blind. "He has a photo of you, so he will know what you look like and find you." Oh, that's OK then, even though I am filtered up to fuck on the pics I gave them to use of me, next thing I know I'll be on an episode of fucking catfish.

"Good morning Miss Rush, how are we this fine morning?" Matt was my lovely boss, always seemed to be happy, never grumpy or mean like most bosses.

He was really tall, like massively tall, lovely kind brown eyes with a few smile lines starting to set in and was a bit of a silver fox to be fair, I could literally talk to him about anything, and he would never judge and always offer the best advice from a man's point of view. I often talked to him and in turn he got to hear about all my crazy dating stories, which always gave him a good laugh if nothing else. "Yeah, I'm really good thanks, had a bit of a mental morning, and a bit stressed now if I'm honest. My mates have set me up on a bloody dating site, I've given them full control, and all I know is that I have a date in the pub tonight with someone called John. I have no clue where he's from, what he looks like, where he works – could be a serial killer for all I know, and they are just sending me off to meet him." Matt sat there quiet for a moment, pondering the information I had just fed to him, then he started giggling to himself, which he tried his best to hide. "Well, Sophie I think it's a bloody great idea, you're too good to be on your own forever and if you're left to your own devices you'd be alone forever. Just go with it and stop overthinking things. Yes, the likelihood is he's not going to be the love of your life, but you don't know if you don't try and failing that, it's all experience for when you meet the right one. Maybe then you won't go mute when you like someone because you'll have this dating game down to a fine art. Can I just ask though whatever possessed you to let your friends take control? I never thought I'd see the day you'd let them take control of your dating life."

As I sat there and digested what he just said, I thought to myself, how in the hell do I word this now, I am going to sound even more like a crazy person than ever before. Let's test him to see if he truly is as non-judgmental as I have always thought, let's push those boundaries. "Matt if I tell you, you have to promise not to laugh at me". Matt nodded with a massive smirk on his face. Right, I thought, here goes. "Well, the other night I was sat with the TV on, and I looked up and I saw him, Finn Holston, I was just totally and utterly gobsmacked for a while, I couldn't even move, he is literally the most amazing man I have ever laid my eyes on. And I know it sounds crazy but right then in that moment I felt something, some sort of connection to him. I just felt like I really had to meet him and speak to him. I then persisted to watch videos of him most of the night and when I googled him and an advertisement came up for tickets to meet him at this year's Comicon up in London. However, tickets are £250. So, I was telling the girls this last night over drinks, when they were nagging away at me about who my plus one would be for Lisa's wedding, and we made a deal. If I let them take control of my dating life by setting up an online dating account and arranging blind dates for me, then they would chip in and get me a ticket to go up to London and meet him. Well of course I obviously, stupidly said yes and have been regretting it ever since, especially now I actually have a date arranged in less than 12 hours' time!"

"Sophie, for the first time in a long time I am speechless, I am genuinely lost for words girl." He sat there thinking for a minute or so and then came out with, "You don't do things by half do you, I think this will be good, because you are so random and really random things always happen to you, I think

this will be a good laugh if nothing else. You never

know you could meet the man of your dreams and

then you can stop obsessing over this Finn or

whatever his bloody name is, you always have liked

to live in a bit of a dream world. How many dates

do you have to go on and when are you going up to

London?" I thought to myself - actually we never

agreed on a number, just a different guy every week.

"We didn't say Matt, no numbers were actually

agreed, so really I could just do a couple for the next

few days and that will be it. We did say however

they would have control for a week, so depends how

many they cram in for me, I'm secretly hoping no

one wants me ha, ha. As for London, it's a few

weeks away yet, I am genuinely so excited, I have

such a good feeling about meeting him, he probably

won't even notice me, but I am trying to be positive."
Shit is that the time, "I have a meeting in three
minutes, so am going to log on before my boss sacks
me." I winked at Matt and off I went.

Lunchtime came quickly, like most men I've been
with! Haven't been this hungry in a long time,
suddenly my crappy chicken salad wasn't as
appealing as I thought it would've been this morning,
I wanted a big fat juicy burger with a shed load of
wedges and chilli cheese bites, no pain no gain.
Mandy, my best friend from work, came and sat
down; she looked really stressed bless her. "You OK
Mand? You look stressed, you need to offload?" As
she sat down, she burst into tears, bless her. "Oh my
god, what's wrong" I gave her a massive cuddle and
wiped her tears away. "Oh Soph, I'm so sorry for
crying, in the bloody canteen of all places, I've just

really had the day from hell today, everything is going wrong, I feel like I have no control over anything and to top it off work has been an absolute nightmare! Mark has been cheating on me – I found out last night, I am just numb, I feel sick to my stomach and don't know what to do." Shit what the hell do I say to that? "My god Mandy, I am so sorry, that's terrible, I want to rip that prick's nut sack off! What are you going to do? Do you want to make a go of things with him, or kick him to the curb?" Mandy sat there and mulled it over for a bit. "I honestly don't think I can even bear to look at him right now, he makes me feel physically sick. Genuinely can't believe he has done this, we have been together 26 years, how could he just throw all of that away?". I just shook my head and gave her a hug, god I would love to rip his cock off and teach that prick a lesson. This is yet another reason why I am happy single, I haven't got the constant worry of someone cheating on me!

Home time came and I was so bloody drained from work and worrying about Mandy, I had totally forgotten about the date, that was until my phone started ringing. "Oh fuck" my guts literally fell out of my ass hole. "Hey, how was work?" Cara sounded chirpier than ever, maybe because she was always happy when she was meddling in my business. I gave off the most enormous sigh "Yeah it was ok, draining, just want to go home, have a hot bath and relax, please tell me the date is cancelled?" Her laugh said it all "No chance, and no you aren't getting out of this one, that is unless you don't want to meet Finn." Well it was worth a try "I know, I know, what time and where?" Cara really couldn't contain her excitement "7 pm in the local, you make sure you let us know progress in the group chat as the evening goes on – we will all wait at yours with the kids, for you to return so you can fill us in straight away."

As 6:30 pm came around and I had thrown around thirty shit fits because nothing I put on looked right and 'I needed new clothes' even though I had more than enough to sink a battleship. Emily and Marie really were at their wits end, this wasn't something that happened now and again, but near enough every time I went out. To be fair to them they were patient with me for the first twenty minutes of me acting like a toddler, but by the time 6:30 pm came they were ready to throw me out of the window.

Mid shit fit, Cara, Lisa, and Kelly turned up to come rescue the kids and make sure I was sent off on my merry way. "Come on Mrs you look hot, get out of that door and meet the man of your dreams" Lisa was shoving me out of the door practically. I pleaded with them one last time, "Can I just see a pic of him first please at least?" Lisa shook her head, shoved me out the door and left me; well that was a bit fucking rude! For a while I contemplated jumping in the car and just buggering off somewhere totally different on my own for a few hours but knowing the girls they have CCTV surveillance set up to watch my every move and the date unfold, bastards.

As I walked into the local pub, it seemed like every man and his dog was out in full force, which was great because I knew everyone, they would all be looking over, winding me up and taking the piss.

Fucking stupid idea this was, why the fuck did I agree to this. Oh, holy shit, someone is coming in....... Oh my god!!! He is fit as fuck, tall, brown hair, brown eyes, nice bit of stubble, his face would make a perfect seat for me. He looked really cock sure and confident, as he walked over to me and flashed me a really cheeky grin. Not going to lie he made my pussy tingle just looking at him, I could imagine what sex with him would be like, dirty as FUCK!

"Well, I'd know who you are anywhere beautiful, nice to meet you Sophie". Oh my god, maybe I wasn't such a catfish after all, also his voice did things to me, maybe the girls actually got it right, fair play they had done an amazing job - I just wanted to get him into bed. "Hi John, it's lovely to meet you, how's your day been?" My god I could hear my voice shaking, I was shitting myself, someone save me right now, I need to get pissed, stat. Hate this part of dating, I literally either clam up and go mute or I get verbal diarrhoea and look like a complete and utter knob. After the first two pints, yes pints which I had practically downed in one, I started loosening up a bit, not literally though, I'm not that much of a dirty bitch - had to at least get past the formalities first. I was so glad I didn't have to worry about driving home, the drinks were flowing well now, as was the conversation. We'd covered off the formalities and the usual boring crap, where do you work? How long have you been single? etc. Now we were on to the interesting stuff, exes. I never went into detail personally for this topic of conversation, always found the ones that had 'psycho' exes were actually the psychos themselves, or if they went on too long slating the ex, they weren't over them. "So, I have been single now for around six years." His eyebrows raised as if to say, 'shit girl, what the hell is wrong with you', cheeky prick. "Through choice might I add, me and the ex-split amicably, he went back to his ex, no drama. I've been on dates just not met anyone I have that connection with, or when I do, they turn out to be absolute lunatics, hence why I'm still on my own." He smiled at me as he was processing this for a while, I could see the cogs turning in his head as if he was contemplating something. "Come on then John your turn." You could see by his face he was shitting bricks. "OK so was with my ex for three years, split up three months ago." Jesus that's fresh, I am waiting for the 'she's nuts' comment, he continued. "There's no hard feelings we went our separate ways, no baggage, so just looking for someone to accept me for me." OK that wasn't so bad - was expecting worse, god he actually seems normal! Maybe it was just the guys I was picking like the girls said. "Listen I really like you, so I want to be honest with you from the off." Oh god here we go what shit show is this now? "The reason we split was because she found out I loved wearing her dirty knickers, she caught me walking around the house in them, I thought she was in work. When she left, I'd gone straight to the washing basket, grabbed a pair and slipped them on, as I was admiring myself in the mirror she walked in and I had to confess all, and here we are, she threw three years down the drain, because I liked her knickers." Gobsmacked, totally and utterly fucking gobsmacked, I had to close my mouth when I came back down to earth. This right here is a prime example of what kind of situations I somehow get myself into. What the fuck am I meant to say to that, not that I am against anyone doing what makes them happy, but I really don't feel comfortable with someone wearing my knickers, what if he didn't wipe his arse properly? He'd get skids in my thongs. "Listen John, I really appreciate the honesty and am all for doing what you want to do, but I don't like to share underwear, plus you'd probably look better in them than me and that would piss me off. I've had a lovely evening getting to know you though, and would love to stay friends if you want?" You could see the disappointment in his face, well fuck I was disappointed too, I was looking forward to getting fucked in a million different ways by this man, and he goes and drops a bollock like that into the conversation. "Yeah, I appreciate that, just gutted as I thought we'd hit it off and you're a beautiful girl, but yeah, it would be nice to stay in contact as friends, if you're sure that's what you want." I nodded and gave him a hug, finished my drink and we said our goodbyes. On the walk home I thought about how to tell the girls and whether to string them along and then drop the bollock like he did? Or do I just get right to it? Well, the girls were so excited about this date, seems only fair to wind them up, teach them a lesson, since they seem to think they can pick the best of the bunch and I am useless.

"Oh my god, how'd it go?" The three of them had pulled out the sofa bed in the living room and drank three bottles of wine that I could see, they were all smiling like Cheshire cats, waiting on my news. "We want every detail, every single one." Lisa blurted out before I could even open my mouth!

"OK, OK, so John was lovely, he walked in, was drop dead gorgeous, which I was not expecting because you wouldn't let me see a pic, which immediately threw me. I literally saw him and had fanny flutters, I just wanted to rip his clothes off there and then, you could just tell he would be a dirty fucker in the bedroom. Anyway, chemistry was amazing, conversation and drinks were flowing, we were both massively flirting with one another. All the signs were good, we got into the ex's conversation and to my surprise all was fine. Until he confessed that he and his ex-split because he liked to wear her dirty knickers! At which point I was pretty taken a-fucking-back if I am honest and made a very sharp exit! So, I don't want to hear off you three ever again, how I am so shit at picking men

and it was just me that had no sense! Now give me
some fucking wine, and let me hear the apologies
from all of you please?" Think they were all as
gobsmacked as I was and stayed silent for a moment,
which in itself was a fucking miracle, then the
laughter started for a solid five minutes, fuckers.
"We're sorry" they all said in tandem, "Listen girls
it's fine, it's yet another experience to add to the list,
now are you lot staying or pissing off home I need
sleep?"

An hour later, once they'd all pissed off, Me, Emily
and Marie led in bed watching a horror film, which
meant there would be no chance of me having the
bed to myself tonight as we'd all be too scared to
sleep separately. I was so grateful for my amazing
kids, friends and family, when all is said and done, I
don't know what I'd do without them. Once the film

had finished and we'd finished scaring the living shit out of each other with "What's that noise?" Or "What the fuck is that over there?" We settled down to sleep and I just lay there relieved that the first date was out of the way, and it was only a few weeks until my journey up to London to see that handsome bastard, Finn. Now that's a nice thought to end my day on.

Chapter 5

Oh Caleb

"What the fuck is that noise?" I woke up to someone hammering on my front door. I shot up and nearly fell over, because I was half asleep and to top it off, I stubbed my fucking toe on the corner of my bedside table. The kids were fast asleep of course, was like waking the dead trying to wake them up. I looked at the time it was 12:30 am "Who the fuck is that at this bloody time of the night?" As I ran down the stairs, looking dishevelled, like I'd been dragged through a hedge backwards, I thought twice about opening the door, especially after the horror I'd just watched. Shit what if I am about to get murdered "Sophie, open the door it's me, I need to see you now, please open the door?" Oh, fuck's sake I knew that voice all too well, my heart just sank, and my stomach turned over like it was a washing machine on a spin cycle. It was Caleb the cock, what the fuck was he doing here now? Hadn't seen him for ages, we'd kept in touch now and again, but it had to have been at least two years since I'd last seen him and that was a highly emotional affair. "Alright, alright just shut the fuck up the kids are sleeping you twat!" As I walked towards the door, I knew what was going to happen, it was what always happened when I saw him, I was going to fuck him and then be filled with regret later. It was impossible to resist him, I don't know why, probably because the sex was so good, but every time I saw him, I just wanted him inside me. I just had to make sure I'd stay strong and not give in to him. Stop thinking with your pussy and stay strong Sophie don't do it, I said to myself.

Fuck, he is as lush as I remember "What do you want? And why the fuck are you hammering on my door at 12:30 in the fucking morning?" Caleb just looked at me with his bright blue eyes and said, "Please let me in, I really need to speak to you." How the hell am I supposed to resist those eyes, I knew deep down what his intentions were and would've put money on the fact he'd heard from one of the boys I was in the pub on a date with someone and now like the prick he is had decided to turn up and royally fuck things up for me. This bloke had a fucking 'Sophie's moving on radar' I swear, every time there was even a slight possibility of me dating someone else, up he would pop, normally via message though to be fair, so he must've been especially worried to pay me a visit at this bloody hour. Unless of course he was here because they had finished things and he wanted to make a go of things with me? And he's turned up to tell me that, like I'd wanted to happen for so long. "Come on then, but don't be fucking ages, I got work in the morning, so I don't have all night." Fuck me, as he walked in, I could smell his aftershave, he smelt absolutely amazing, he was wearing my favourite aftershave, he knew what that smell did to me. I wanted him right now but managed to resist and be strong, he'd only been here two seconds and already I was imagining him being inside me. "So, what do you want that couldn't wait until a decent time of the fucking day?" He looked at me with such wanting eyes. He hesitated for a second or two before pinning me up against the wall and said "You, you're what I want." As he grabbed me and kissed me, I could feel the electricity coursing through my veins, I could feel my pussy aching for him to be buried deep inside me "fuck, stop." I pushed him away briefly, I tried OK, didn't last long but it's the thought that counts right? That was until I gave in, grabbed him and kissed him like I wanted him with every fibre of my being. As I licked and bit his neck, he stroked his hand up my leg towards my pussy, and I felt just how hard is cock was through his jeans, against my skin. I waited with anticipation as he pulled my knickers off, he slid two fingers deep inside me and I moaned loudly in his ear with pleasure. "Fuck, I've missed you Soph and your soaking wet pussy." He whispered as I arched my back to let him get deeper. I reached down and unbuckled his jeans and fell to my knees, Mmmm there it was, the thing I missed the most about Caleb - his perfect cock. Then I licked the pre-cum off his throbbing bell end and gave just a little suck as I looked up at him to tease him, pushed him to the floor and sat on his face. I put his cock in my mouth and sucked him off as I rubbed my pussy on his tongue and rode his face. I could feel the pressure mounting as he massaged my clit with his tongue. No one pleasured me the way he did, he knew every inch of me and what I needed. He genuinely was the best I'd ever had; I'd never be bored of him. Grinding on his face I couldn't hold it anymore and I gave into the pleasure and moaned like fuck as I felt the release when I came, fuck I'd missed him too. He pulled me off him, onto the floor and hovered above me licking my mouth so I could taste myself on his tongue "You taste lush, don't you?" I just let out another moan. "I want to feel you inside me Caleb" and with that he slowly slid his rock-hard cock inside me, and I let out a moan "I take it by how wet you are that you missed me too." I fucking had missed him, especially now with him inside me I realized just how much. After I'd cum no less than five times he gave in. "Fuck I've missed you and your tight, wet pussy, I'm going to cum, where do you want it baby, where do you want it, tell me." Truth was I wanted it everywhere, I couldn't get enough of him. "I want you to cum all over my tongue." Just so I could swallow it all. "OK baby cum for me first one more time and I'll cum all over it and you can taste me." Fuck, I felt it building again, his cock penetrated me perfectly as he licked and sucked my hard nipples and I dug my nails in his back "Fuck me harder Caleb, I love how your cock feels inside me." He moaned with pleasure and I gave into it and climaxed again, this time all over his hard cock.

Fuck I felt thoroughly fucked, so much so my legs were shaking and felt like jelly. I got up and knelt before him and looked up at him with my big, brown, wanting eyes "Cum for me, I want it in my mouth and all over my tongue." As I licked my cum off his bell end, I began to suck his cock and played with his balls as he moaned. I took his cock out of my mouth and wanked him off as I stuck my tongue out. He came like fuck all over it, I sucked off the remaining cum on his cock and swallowed it down.

The most satisfied I'd felt in a long time, I sat up and put my tits away, pulled my night dress back down and found my knickers. Shit, I'd got so caught up in all of that I didn't ask the question "You are single now then I take it?" Me like the stupid idiot I was, thought he had split with his girlfriend and wanted to be with me, which would've explained why he had turned up here not just messaged me. "Well not exactly, Sophie I had to see you, I miss you so much." The look on my face said it all, I was fucking livid, more with myself for being such a dumb ass and giving into him yet again. "Are you fucking kidding me, my god I am so fucking stupid, get dressed and get the fuck out of my house, NOW!" Caleb looked like he was about to cry, for a second I felt sorry for him, I soon snapped out of that! "Please Sophie, just hear me out for a second? It's not what you think." I nodded and immediately regretted it, what the hell was I doing, he could literally talk his way out of any situation. "I can't stop thinking about you, literally 24/7 you are on my mind. And when I got sent that picture of you and some guy earlier from Gary in the pub, I lost my head, I've been sitting there not knowing what to do with myself, I wasn't going to come over. I tried my best to stay away, but I couldn't, I had to see you and tell you how I felt. I can't leave her, but I love you and I want you." And there it is, what a twat I turned out to be! What was he expecting, for me to be his mistress? "You are joking right Caleb? I mean like literally joking, there's no way you can be serious right now. So, it was exactly as I thought, you'd heard that I was on a date and thought shit I don't like her with someone else, let's go fucking ruin it for her! I don't want her, but I don't want anyone else to have her! Where is your girlfriend in all of this? Where does she think you've gone, cause it's not the pub or the shop, it's ONE IN THE FUCKING MORNING. God I actually hate you right now, like so fucking much, so much so if your face was on fire, I'd put it out with a fork!" I could feel myself filling up, how much could this prick actually hurt me, I was more pissed off at myself for letting this happen again, he just sat there like a fucking plum. "Please just leave and never fucking contact me again, and I mean EVER, or I will fucking tell her and ruin your life, see how you fucking like it, prick. Get your shit and leave. Here, I'll help you." I grabbed his shoes and his coat and threw them out of the front door and he soon followed. "I'm really sorry Sophie, I do love you, please don't be like this." Seriously, what the fuck did he expect? "Just fuck off Caleb, and once you have done that, fuck off again, you don't love me, you can't, you don't even know what love is."

After I'd slammed the door I fell to the floor and burst into floods of tears. God, he made me so angry, these were angry tears, not sad tears. Right there and then I made a vow to myself to never see or speak to that man again as long as I am on this earth. I pulled myself up off the floor and wiped away the tears that were rolling down my face and took myself off to bed. Truth was I had cried way too much over this man and from this moment on I wasn't prepared to cry anymore! As far as I was concerned, before we were amicable; now we far fucking from it, and truthfully, I could never move on properly whilst I was still in contact with him, as it never felt truly done. Tonight, as painful as it was, made me draw a line under the whole fucked up situation, tomorrow is a new day with new possibilities. As I lay there, I began to calm down. My eyes we're stinging; I closed them and went straight off to sleep.

6:30 am I was awoken by my alarm, "Holy fuck, I'm too tired for this shit today." As I walked into the bathroom, I caught a glimpse of myself in the mirror, and fuck I looked rough as fuck, like I had been hit by a bus. "What the fuck am I meant to do with my face today?" My eyes were really swollen and puffy from crying over that twat, they looked like piss holes in the snow. I don't even think the power of makeup will fix this today. As I stood in the shower, I gave myself a good talking to; from this day forward, I was not falling for any man's shit ever again, least of all that prick's! I wish I could be a lesbian or completely celibate so I wouldn't have to deal with all this shit I seem to attract from men; unfortunately, though, I fucking loved cock. Can't believe I even let him in last night, I knew it was about as clever as that woman who had put popping candy in her vagina!

Once my shower was over and I'd sorted my hair and face out, I actually didn't look so bad, thankfully, at least I wouldn't have to explain to everyone why I'd obviously been bawling my eyes out; either that or I had a severe case of conjunctivitis or pink eye. As I dropped Emily off at school, we had a good sing-song to a bit of Ariana Grande, 'Thank you next' - of course, I had to turn it down as we approached school though, or I'd embarrass her. I wasn't working in the office today, thankfully as I am sure the way things are going pig man would be there waiting to pounce. I spent the day at some training course - to be honest I couldn't tell you what it was all about, as I was so tired, I couldn't pay attention, it took all of my strength just to stay awake.

Today I didn't need a mood ring, people could see by my face that I was far from approachable. I think the trainer had just given up on me after about thirty minutes of him trying to get me to participate, I wasn't the most forthcoming, which wasn't like me, normally couldn't shut me up at things like this. I needed to snap out of this mood pronto, I couldn't let him affect my work. I just couldn't wait to get home and chill out, after the day I had it was needed so I picked up the phone at lunchtime and rang Cara to tell her I wasn't meeting anyone this evening after what had happened last night. Once she stopped shouting and bawling at me for what I'd done, she asked whether I was OK. Of course, I wasn't but I just assured her that I was, and I just wanted to be left alone, just for today to get my shit together. I was better coping on my own with shit like this, I hated everyone fussing over me - it just made me worse. She couldn't exactly say no after everything that had happened in the last 24 hours and just said "If you need me you know where I am." Thank god, I'd got out of that. Emily and Marie will no doubt cheer me up later, my kids were my world and if anyone could make me smile, laugh and forget about all of the crap, it was them.

As we were sitting there eating a massive pizza for tea, watching god knows what crap on the TV, Marie comes out with this cracker "My birthday is usually on a Tuesday?" Oh, fuck's sake, me and Emily (who's 10) looked at each other in total disbelief. I just put my head in my hands and pissed myself for a solid five minutes. She remained straight faced and kept asking why we were laughing. Marie always came out with statements like this and had everyone in hysterics. I remember the once I had to leave work because she was hysterically crying and screaming on the phone. She'd let herself into the house after school and could hear talking. So, she grabbed a knife and followed the voice, she went upstairs and into Emily's bedroom. The talking was coming from there, she opened the door and as it happened it was one of Emily's dolls. She ran out of the house faster than a rat up a drainpipe. Well, I was immediately in receipt of a very distressing phone call, so distressing in fact, Matt sent me home, he could hear her in hysterics on the end of the phone. She was adamant she would not go back into the house until I came home to rescue her from the possessed doll. Instances such as this were a regular occurrence, she was one on her own; it was bloody embarrassing though when I had to explain to people that I had to leave work early because there was a possessed doll talking to my daughter at home. Thankfully I never had anything happen like this yet with Emily. Both my daughters looked so much alike, but yet they had totally different personalities.

Once me and Emily had recovered from the laughing fit, we explained that her birthday was on a different day every year. Marie looked confused, shrugged her shoulders, and swiftly changed the subject.

Marie was really intelligent, just had no common sense and was one of the kindest people you could meet; she was always happy and would light up a room whenever she entered. Emily was a budding artist and was crazy about art in general, she was bloody good at it too. She was really streetwise as well, unlike her sister (even though she was a lot younger) and she was a sensitive soul. They got on for the most part, until Marie would try winding Emily up. Emily would take it for a while and then she would snap, and when she snapped, she snapped! They were playing on the xbox one day - Marie beat her on the game and was taunting her, laughing in her face and rubbing it right in. I could see Emily's temper boiling up then smack, she hit Marie in the face with the remote and walked off.

Once we'd finished our pizza, we snuggled down with a blanket on the sofa - next I knew I woke myself up snoring like a warthog. The kids were filming me, the little sods. "You best not show that to anyone!" I grabbed them and gave them a massive cuddle "Right come on Emily, it's your bedtime, and mine, clearly. Love you Marie, no showing anyone that video now, promise?" Once she'd finished laughing, she said "I won't mam I promise, I love you too!"

What a long day! I got into fresh clean bedding, with my freshly shaved legs, it was absolute heaven. I put a bit of mindfulness on, and that's the last I can remember.

Chapter 6

On the Eve

As my alarm went off, I was feeling alive today, unlike the shower of shit that was yesterday; I also didn't scare myself when I looked in the mirror either, which was always a bonus. I was in an amazing mood, even after all of that shit that went down with Caleb, I'd felt like a weight had been lifted and I was finally at a place where I was ready to move on from that chapter in my life. I'd been so hung up on him for so long, I hadn't realised I was subconsciously shutting myself off from ever moving on with anyone else. I think I always held out hope that he felt how I did and that one day he would 'come to his senses' and realise he wanted to be with me more than anything. Now I could see if he loved me as much as he said he always did, he would've moved mountains to be with me, instead of stringing me along and fobbing me off. At the end of the day all he ever wanted was that mind blowing sex from me, which don't get me wrong was amazing, but it was so much more than that to me. Today though it was as if someone had flicked a switch in my mind, and I'd woken up from that 'hypnosis' I was under, and I'd finally got it into my thick skull what Cara, Kelly and Lisa had been telling me all this time. I was free of his magic now and it felt amazing, I felt like a whole new woman, I felt like I could start a whole new life – it felt absolutely amazing.

As I was getting ready for work Lisa rang me "Good morning Lis how are you this fine morning? I'm just getting ready for work, I am on a mission from this day forward, never to let that fucktard into my life again." She started giggling and sounded excited for me "Oh Soph, you have no idea how long we've all been waiting to hear you say that! I was ringing to check in on you, I know you wanted to be left alone yesterday, but I've been worried sick after Cara told us what had happened. That said, the kids are going to their dad's for the weekend, and I know you'll be all alone, so we decided to book a girl's trip this weekend to cheer you up!" OMG these girls were the best friends ever, they were always there for me, I felt like crying now bless her. "Oh wow, Lisa thank you so much, I honestly don't know what to say to that, but I can't wait! A girl's trip is exactly what I need after the last few days. Where are we going, just so I know what to pack for?" This was just what I needed, some time with the girls, to let loose and unwind, let my hair down, this would be the medicine I needed. "Well, how does Amsterdam sound?" Holy fuck!!! "It sounds bloody amazing, you've made my day, thank you all so much for arranging this, I'm just in shock, I best get packing then ahhhhhhhh."

I knew when I'd opened my eyes today was going to be a bloody good day and so far, it couldn't have been better. Couldn't wait to get to work and be back on top form. I know all work is shit but I really do love my job, as much as someone could enjoy a job I suppose.

Once I'd finished nagging Emily and Marie to hurry up and get ready for school, I broke the news to them that I was off to Amsterdam for the weekend with the girls. "Can I come?" Emily looked at me with her puppy dog eyes, god how was I going to put this without it kicking off now. The kids never liked me going away without them, which is fair enough, it wasn't something I did often because I felt guilty going anywhere without them, but I needed this trip. "I'm sorry sweetheart, but mam needs to get away with the girls, for some rest and relaxation. You'll be at dads all weekend though which will be lovely, you can spend some time with him and I'm sure he will spoil you." Emily looked so sad, bless her. I felt that horrible guilty feeling, which any mother feels when she is actually doing something for herself. But at that moment I remembered what I was told years before, 'you need you time in order to be on top form for your children'. It's so easy to be 'mam' all the time, it's so easy to lose your identity. I'd cancelled so many nights out in the past because of the guilt I felt, but I needed a break now and then too. "Mam you will have an amazing time, it's just what you need, just please behave? Don't go getting into any stupid situations, like getting arrested, remember you are in a foreign country." Christ, who is the parent here? Marie did think she was the parent a lot of the time, she liked to boss me around. But it was always coming from a good place, she was trying to look out for me. I'd had Marie at a young age; we'd gone through so much together we were more like sisters than mother and daughter. Which for the most part was brilliant, we had a lovely relationship, but when it came to disciplining her, it was extremely challenging as sometimes she didn't take me seriously. To be fair she was a good kid, so I didn't have to discipline her much anyway, thankfully.

Once I'd dropped the girls off, it was time to get the music blasting for the drive to work. Today's music of choice was Celine Dion, 'It's all coming back to me now'. This was a belter! I waved my arms around and sang at the top of my lungs "I finished crying in the instant that you left, and I can't remember when or where or how". I must've looked like a crazy person, but I didn't give a fuck, I felt empowered as fuck and wanted to sing it from the roof tops, if people didn't like it then bollocks to them! I was an independent bad ass bitch, and I was never going to sell myself short again, not for anyone!

Nothing could bring me down, not even the sight of pig man right in front of me, waiting for me to vacate the vehicle. "Here we go" I muttered to myself as I got out of the car, "Good morning Nigel, how are you today?" He looked shocked as it was

me that had opened the lines of communication; dear

lord I hope he didn't take that the wrong way. "Well

hello Miss Rush" Oh for fuck's sake, he had a

stringy bit of white in the corner of his mouth again,

what even is that? I'm sure he has a boner, it just

caught my eye, Christ on a bike, he's got a boner.

As I looked back up, I made eye contact with him.

"Sorry to be rude, but I am in hell of a rush, I am late

for a meeting, hope you have a nice day!" I grabbed

my shit and left so quickly he didn't have the time to

say anything. Well clearly, I'd made someone's day

today; god I hope he doesn't go for a wank now, I

need to get those thoughts out of my head, now! I

don't know why my mind wanders in all these

bloody directions, it was horrible, I'd think about

something, then I'd make myself feel sick, just couldn't help myself, it was an affliction I had.

As I got into the office, it was very quiet, I was the first one in, which wasn't nice as I needed to tell someone what just happened down in the carpark ASAP. Hope Mandy was ok, I text her yesterday and hadn't heard back off her, though that wasn't unusual from her, she was useless at replying - it was pointless her having a phone to be fair. Wonder if she's kicked that useless wanker to the kerb or decided to take him back? I hope she kicked him to the kerb, he treated her like shit most of the time anyway. As I see it this is her perfect way out of the shitty relationship, as scary as it must be being with someone for that long. I don't see how a relationship can ever recover from someone cheating, you would never trust that person again.

Whatever she's decided will be right for her and I will support her of course. "Good Morning Sophie, nice of you to join us to do some work today!" Matt joked as he walked in the door. "Afternoon boss, yes I just couldn't stay away for long, miss the place too much. All jokes aside, that bloody training course was an absolute pile of wank. Oh, and you'd never guess what happened this morning? I saw pig man in the car park, spoke to him and caught sight of his boner, I'm still trying to get that image out of my head!" I think he pissed himself laughing for a solid five minutes before he looked at me like he was going to burst with excitement. "Never bloody mind that, what happened on the bloody date with John wasn't it?" Oh god, so much had gone on since then I had totally forgotten about that date. "Christ, I haven't seen you for one day and so much has gone on. Well, where to start, so John was lovely; he walked in, was drop dead gorgeous, which I was not expecting because the girls wouldn't let me see a pic, which immediately threw me. I literally saw him and had fanny flutters, I just wanted to rip his clothes off there and then, you could just tell he would be a dirty fucker in the bedroom. Anyway, chemistry was amazing, conversation and drinks were flowing, we were both massively flirting with one another. All the signs were good, we got into the ex's conversation and to my surprise all was fine. Until he confessed that he and his ex-split because he liked to wear her dirty knickers! I was just in total and utter shock, I had to physically close my mouth. It's funny now to look back on but at the time I was a bit gutted, I was imagining getting fucked by him in fifty different ways and he goes and tells me that."

Matt's face was a picture, he stood in shock for a few seconds before he burst out into hysterics. Looking less than impressed I said, "I'm not telling you the rest now, it gets worse, it must've been the full moon or something." He pouted "Please I won't laugh anymore I promise, it's just you couldn't make this shit up. I honestly don't think I have ever known anyone to have the luck with men that you do, and you didn't even pick this one, so this one is your friend's fault. Come on tell me, please?" Bless him, he loved the fact his life would never be as crazy as mine, but loved hearing about all of the adventures, and believe me there were way too many to even talk about. "Ok, well the next part isn't funny, more annoying than anything, but it's fine now, I have woken up, put my big girl pants on and am well and truly over it. So, after I got back, when

I ran away from my date, the girls went home after I'd filled them in of course and I went to bed and watched a horror film with the kids. Next thing I knew it was 12:30 am and someone was hammering fuck out of the door, it was none other than Caleb the cock. Of course, at the sight of him I had to fuck him, without thinking of the consequences. After we'd had the most mind-blowing sex, it turned out he was still with his Mrs and wasn't single like I had so wrongly assumed. I shouted and bawled, threw him out and cried my eyes out, went to bed and decided after being a miserable cow yesterday that today was a new chapter in my life, and it was time to properly move on and forget about that prick, and here I am." He looked at me like he felt sorry for me, hated it when people did that, it made me feel stupid. "Oh god Sophie, well at least now you have come to realise, he's not the one for you now – only took you years. Listen this is good, especially if you're feeling really good about it, you've definitely done the right thing in all of this. And you still got amazing sex out of it, even if it ended badly. You deserve so much better and the sooner you realise that and start putting yourself first the bloody better. As I keep telling you, it'll happen when you least expect it and no doubt with the person you least expect it to be. That's what happened with me and Anna, and I couldn't be happier with her." Matt had had a hell of a time of it with his ex, she truly was a poisonous bitch, he never thought he'd meet anyone again. Thankfully he met Anna on a night out and they clicked instantly, I was really happy for him. "On the plus side, Lisa rang me this morning, worried sick after my shenanigans the other night and told me we're all off to Amsterdam this weekend for a girl's weekend away. It made my bloody day; it's going to be absolute fucking carnage." At that moment the phone rang and interrupted our conversation - bit rude really, how dare someone expect me to work, I'm trying to talk about my social life and get excited for the weekend. We both pouted and waved at each other as I picked up the phone to the inconsiderate customer.

As 9 am approached, Mandy arrived. To my astonishment she looked absolutely bloody fantastic! Not that she looked like shit before but being cheated on looks good on her fair play, she's had a hell of a glow up. "Well good sexy lady! You're looking absolutely gorgeous! How are you doing, you didn't answer my messages again, I was worried?" Fucking bitch, I always look like shit after something totally shit happens, I either put on weight, look like death or have a breakout of spots all over my face. Never have I ever had a glow up after a breakup. "Sorry I haven't replied, I've had that many messages and it was doing my head in, you know me, I'd rather speak in person. But do you know what Soph, I feel fucking amazing. I got rid of that prick two days ago and so far, it's been the best thing I have ever done. The house is clean, like all the time, I'm not picking up all that lazy prick's mess, I'm not being spoken to like I am a total piece of shit and I get the bed to myself. After our chat the other day, I went home and as soon as I saw his face, I felt physically sick at the thought of what he'd done, I knew I couldn't take him back. He wasn't happy about it though. First, he was sad and tried manipulating me, then he got angry with me when he realised he couldn't control the situation. I really wish he'd done this years ago so I wouldn't have wasted all this time with such a cock." I was made up for her; if anyone deserved to be happy it was her. "I am so bloody happy for you Mandy, you deserve happiness and who knows, maybe now you will meet someone that actually deserves such an amazing person like you, just don't take no shit and enjoy every moment." I then went on to fill her in on all of my drama from the last few days that she'd missed out on, which of course gave her a good laugh - glad my misfortunes amused people.

Home time came and I couldn't get home quick enough, I was on a mission to get everything packed tonight in readiness for AMSTERDAM tomorrow. First though, I had persuaded Emily and Marie to come and see Finn's new film with me tonight. As long as they could have all the snacks they wanted they were up for watching anything. "So, mam what's this film you're dragging me and Emily out to watch tonight then, is it actually any good or are we just going because that Finn guy you're obsessed with is in it?" God she was so hard done by bless her. "It's had really good reviews actually, and please just humour me, he is bloody gorgeous! Even if the film is shit, we can have fun looking at him for a few hours." Once I'd re-mortgaged my house to buy the entire contents of the cinema's snack section, we were seated ready for the film. I was so bloody excited for the next few weeks. So much had happened in the last few days, but the next few weeks were going to be absolutely mental, bring it on.

My god he really is the most handsome bastard on this planet, and that smile wow! How am I going to cope when I meet him, what if I faint? Or worse, make a dick of myself. I knew the likelihood of him even looking at me in that way was basically single to none. But I could fantasize right? I kept thinking, what if we meet and bang fall in love like in the films, what if he sees me and thinks, fuck I want her, like I think about him? I basically spent the entire film not really paying attention and imagining what it was going to be like when we met. Imagining his tongue in my mouth, all over me in fact – had to reign myself in and fucking behave myself at least until I got home and went to bed.

Film over, and the kids seemed to enjoy it too, not for the same reasons I did though. We decided to go and have a few games of bowling before I left them tomorrow for the whole weekend as they kept reminding me. The guilt trip didn't work this time though, I was bloody going, I needed a break away from everything, for my own sanity and my mental health.

Once Emily had kicked our asses at every game, literally all of them, we headed home. We all went to bed, and as my head hit the pillow, I contemplated fucking myself, however my body had other ideas though and I fell fast asleep. I did however have the most fucking amazing dream about Finn, so amazing I came in my sleep and it woke me up. I went back to sleep quickly to try and get back into the same dream, but I can't remember anything from there on.

Chapter 7

Girl's trip

"It's Friday!" I sang at the top of my lungs, at precisely 6am, sure my neighbours absolutely fucking hated my guts, but guess what? I didn't give a fuck this morning. "Oh, we're going to Amsterdam" I sang to the tune of 'we're going to Ibiza' by the Vengaboys. Pretty sure my kids hated me right now as well, the death glare was a bit of a giveaway as I entered their rooms to open their curtains and wake the little darlings for school. "Come on my beautiful children, fruit of my loins." I knew they hated it when I said that. "Mam stop being so fucking disgusting and shut my curtains, I know you're excited but please leave me alone." Marie was an absolute joy in the mornings; Emily however was normally good as gold getting up and was for the most part, happy. "That's not a very nice way to speak to your mother Marie." I quickly left her room before she launched something at my skull - couldn't afford to be injured today, nothing was stopping me going on my girl's trip.

I quickly took to our WhatsApp group chat to send a voice note "Good morning you sexy bitches, WE'RE GOING TO AMSTERDAM TODAY! Get up fuckers! I need someone to be excited with me. Yes, I know it's early and no I don't give a fuck, what time are you picking me up for the airport? Can we go right now? I know we're not flying until 1pm but let's get in the departure lounge and get wankered." They were going to kill me, I always got over excited and had absolutely no patience whatsoever. "Fuck off" Lisa was first to respond -

that was a bit harsh. "Remember what happened on the last girl's trip because you got over excited and ended up absolutely bolloxed, and shagged your boss's mate? I'm sure you don't want a repeat of that, Miss Rush so calm your tits, bitch." Thanks Cara, she had to bloody bring that up didn't she. It was a long story, and as I've said previously, I don't do one night stands (usually) even though I seem to have, given most of my stories are about them. Anyway, we had gone up to Scotland for the rugby. Matt had said to me prior to this that his mate "Big Jeff" was going and to keep a look out for him and say hi if I came across him, which in itself was highly unlikely given the amount of people going. First night I didn't meet anyone as I was too paralytic, but on the second day at Murrayfield I was literally sat right bloody next to him. Anyway, we got chatting and realised who each other was, took a few selfies and sent them to Matt, showing off that we were up in Scotland, watching the rugby and getting pissed whilst he was at home. After the best game of rugby I've seen in a long time, we all went out for drinks, and of course we were celebrating the Welsh victory, and things got out of hand. At this point I had a job to see straight, I grabbed hold of 'Big Jeff' and stuck my tongue down his throat. I bet it was the worst kiss ever, but truth be told I can't even remember it, this is just what the girls have told me. I then went on to say to Jeff "I'm going to fuck the shit out of you later!" - My god I feel mortified just repeating this. Anyway, that's all I know as I couldn't remember, and the girls only saw up to the point where I dragged him out of there and back to his hotel room. I remember waking up and wanting to disappear up my own asshole.

I rolled over and was met by him gazing at me. He'd had a good time clearly as his cock was hard again and he didn't want me to leave. I made my excuses and I got out of there ASAP, and back to my own room where I was met with the girls ripping into me all fucking day. They showed me videos of me acting a total twat the night before, I hate that I can't remember and for a good reason, let's keep it that way - I don't want to feel bloody worse!

After I'd returned, I had to face Matt at work. Now he'd not been there long, two or three months maximum, so I was literally shitting fucking bricks. I knew why they called him 'Big Jeff' now anyway, I was walking like I'd shit myself; this was days after and I was still sore as fuck, Jesus. Anyway, long story short, Matt came in and tried to wind me up for a bit, telling me that Jeff was beside himself as he just wanted to see me, and I was blocking his calls and messages and that he couldn't believe I would do this and how unprofessional it was to shag the boss's mate. I was absolutely fucking mortified, and for the first time in a long time, fucking speechless! I literally felt like crying, I thought to myself, 'this is the day I lose my job.'

As I opened my mouth to try and talk my way out of it, he started pissing himself, and right there and then I didn't know whether to hug him or punch the fucker in the face. So yes, Cara was right, I didn't want a repeat of last time, I was going to take my time and pace myself, or at least try not to get in fucking dreadful situations. "Fuck sake, yes thanks for that Cara, can always rely on you to remind me of all the twat moments I've had. All jokes aside what time are we going so I know when to be ready?" I sounded like all the excitement had gone out of my voice "Don't be sad, I was only winding you up, we will pick you up at 10, be ready beautiful." I felt better already, I hated not having a plan to work towards.

I was ready by 8am, I'd dropped the kids off, and we'd said our goodbyes. I was bored fuckless now, so I stuck some music on and sang and danced my heart out, imagining I was some hot badass bitch on a stage somewhere: that took up like thirty minutes. What the fuck was I going to do for another hour and a half? I know I'll watch videos of Mr Finn Holston for a bit, if anything he can take my mind off the fact, I have an eternity to wait; now where's my dildo?

By the time 10 am came around, I had came no less than five times. I'd had a lovely morning, and had a lovely glow about me, now I was ready to go.

I had a text they were on route, woo-hoo about bloody time too! So, I grabbed my stuff and waited outside, not that I was eager or anything ha, ha. As they came down the street, they had the music blasting and were beeping the horn like crazy people. My neighbour came out and said 'who the hell is that?' looking pissed off, so I apologised on their behalf, I got into the car and acted like a twat too.

We literally spent the whole journey to the airport singing at the top of our lungs and dancing, how the fuck we didn't die on route I don't know as we nearly veered off the road a few times. Thankfully though, we got to Bristol airport nice and safe and sound.

As soon as we'd checked ourselves in, we headed to the bar for a few cheeky drinks before the impending flight, where it felt like strapping a rocket to our arse. This was a requirement if we were ever going anywhere, I had to fly - I fucking hated flying, was more the taking off than anything, I wasn't too bad once I was up there or coming down. Once we'd boarded that rocket, the old nerves were starting to set in again, but luckily Kelly was a calming influence so she sat next to me and took my mind off it as much as she could.

As expected, I shit my pants (not literally) as we took off and had to hold back the urge to shout out "We're all going to die! We're all going to die!" But once that horrific bit was over, I was fine and for the first time ever, I fell asleep and they had to wake me up when we were landing, not only that I was dribbling on Kelly's arm and all up my face, so that was nice. They also informed me I was snoring like a pig, wonderful. Once I'd wiped the dribble from all over the right side of my face, the wheels touched that tarmac and I felt relief as everyone on the plane started clapping, I didn't know if they were clapping because the plane had landed safely or if they were happy to be getting away from the sound of my snores.

Chapter 8

Sexy surprise, drugs and rock and roll

As we finally got our bags from the airport, after waiting what felt like hours, we were on route to the hotel. On our way we were making our plans for the weekend. Cara had put an itinerary together which looked extremely stressful, due to the sheer amount she had squeezed into such a small time. "Not being funny Cara, it was a lovely thought to put all this together, but I think we should at least have one evening of bloody enjoying ourselves rather than just sightseeing the whole time. I say we get settled into our rooms now, unpack, get dressed up, go out and relax, then go sightseeing tomorrow, Sophie, Kelly what do you think? Back me up here." Lisa was giving us the evil glare as she said this, to be honest she didn't need to threaten me I wanted a bloody good night out. "I agree with Lisa, after the week I've had I need to unwind and let loose a bit, let's just go out get pissed and let our hair down". Lisa looked pleased with herself that I'd taken her side. "Yep, sorry Cara I agree with Kelly and Sophie, we all deserve a good old piss up, plus who knows we may even find Sophie a man". Fuck's sake even on holiday they don't give up, they were right though, who knows, the man of my dreams could be here in a bar. Cara didn't look too pleased, but couldn't disagree as majority rules, "Ok we will do it your way, let's go out get shit faced, then take in a bit of culture tomorrow" she said as she pouted.

Once we'd all freshened up, we got ready to some music, it was a bit of a mixed bag as we all love different music, had a bit of RNB, Rock, Reggae and some dance on the go. We drank two bottles of rose champagne, which went down a bit too nicely, I was already feeling fucked, and we'd not even left the hotel room yet. We spent a good hour or so dancing round the bedroom, thinking we were right sexy mother fuckers, this was thanks to the bubbles going to our heads. "Right come on girls, let's go get some coffee" Kelly said with a wink. What the fuck was that all about? "I don't fucking want coffee thanks, I want a fuck load of alcoholic beverages!" I think I showed I was less than impressed by the crap that just came out of Kelly's mouth, was she taking the piss or what? Crazy bitch. "Ok, ok, let's find a bar then, maybe we can grab coffee later." What was this woman's obsession with coffee? Maybe she thought she was being funny? I just didn't get the joke to be perfectly honest.

The first bar we went to, I can remember quite well, that was until all of the shots of tequila hit me! Five shots and multiple beers in, I think we all went a bit overboard too soon, we had all got so excited, this often happened when we went out on the town and usually it ended with me making a complete and utter dick of myself. Cara was being sick in the toilet; Kelly and I were dancing, and Lisa was looking after Cara. If I saw Cara spew, I'd probably be sick too and that would no doubt lead to me pissing myself, as I'd had two children my bladder couldn't handle that kind of pressure. I didn't have a change of clothes with me for that and didn't fancy walking back to the hotel with pissy pants, so I opted to stay as far away from that as possible.

As me and Kelly were dancing, two crazy fuckers came up to us and started grinding up against us, which of course we found hysterical because we were pissed. "Hey sexy ladies, I'm Johan and this is Bert, what's your name?" Here we go, this will no doubt be our entertainment for a few hours sorted. "Hi, we're Sophie and Kelly." I said, giving them a cheeky wink, egging them on further.

They weren't bad looking to be fair, Johan was really big and muscly and blonde with a beard, reminded me of a Viking, would definitely throw you over his shoulder and take you to bed, I wouldn't mind a bit of that right now. And Bert was a bit of alright too, he wasn't as big as his friend, but he had something about him, he looked naughty, like he would ruin you in the bedroom. "Wow beautiful names, for beautiful ladies, may we buy you a drink?" "Fuck yeah" we never say no to free drinks, "Two beers please?"

Johan and Bert returned, beers in hand at the same time Cara and Lisa appeared after being sick in the toilet for the last ten minutes. I introduced everyone and the boys got two more drinks in for Cara and Lisa, fair play they must've wanted to get their ends away. Me and Johan had a cheeky snog or two before the girls decided they wanted to move onto the next bar. They spend forever trying to find me a man, when I find one, they want to pull me away from him, twats. We exchanged numbers and we went on our merry way to find the next bar. "Girls, why were you so insistent we move onto another bar? All you do is nag me to find a man, I find someone hot on a night out and you do everything you can to get me away from him? What the fuck are you playing at? I was enjoying myself?" All three girls started laughing simultaneously, when

Cara said "Sophie, you have your beer goggles on, trust us we did you a favour in 'dragging you away', you'll thank us when I show you a picture in the morning when you're sober that you've not taken him home and have woken up next to him in bed, filled with regret, trying to get rid of him." I was confused, both men were hot as far as I was concerned, I wasn't that pissed surely? Why do my eyes deceive me so badly? Fuckers! "Seriously girls? I genuinely thought they looked like Vikings, I'm going to take it easy now the rest of the night, god knows what I'd end up with." I really needed to slow down the pace or I'd be fucked.

"Right, Sophie, we're doing the one thing we have to do in Amsterdam, let's go have some coffee and more importantly some cake." You could hear the excitement in Kelly's voice, and suddenly the penny dropped, she was talking about marijuana all along not bloody coffee. God I could be so thick sometimes. Truth be told, I was dreading this, I didn't like the stuff, I'd tried it before when I was younger and all it did was make me ill, I couldn't stop throwing up. Think I will just let them crack on and I'll pretend to eat the stuff. "Christ come on then, I give up with you lot, let's go have some cake to shut Kelly up at least."

There were quite a few places serving space cakes and mushrooms, but the girls finally decided on one that looked 'safest' and we went in and ordered a load of cakes, no mushrooms this time though thankfully, that could go wrong very quickly. Cara, Kelly and Lisa practically inhaled their bloody cakes, Jesus these girls were on a fucking mission. I was breaking bits off mine, pretending to eat it, then throwing it on the floor when they weren't looking; so far, I was getting away with it. "Come on Sophie eat the rest, you're taking ages, we all ate ours ages ago." Cara was nagging me again, fucking drug pusher. "To be honest girls this cake is foul, I'm struggling. I feel like I'm going to be sick." All three rolled their eyes, but didn't push any further, thankfully. "Girls I don't feel any different, shall we get some mushrooms? Only the mild ones?" Lisa clearly wanted to get absolutely obliterated tonight. "Let that kick in first you crazy fuck." I was actually being the sensible one right now, this never happened, usually I was the stupid twat. "Fuck that, miss sensible, I'm getting some fucking mushrooms." There was no stopping Lisa tonight, off she went to go get her drugs, tonight was going to be entertaining if nothing else, especially considering I hadn't had anything so wouldn't be on the same level as them.

All three of the silly twats were chucking the mushrooms down their throat, and I just sat back and waited for the craziness to begin. It was 3pm and we were all smashed and now they were off their chops too. Cara stood up suddenly and said, "Let's go for a walk." Fuck me this would be a nightmare, how the hell would I keep all three of them in check? I swear to god, if one of them falls in the river or something like that, I will kill them myself! So far so good, we were all walking at the same pace and everyone was quite sensible. "Fuuuuuccccckkkkk." Lisa said in slow motion "Can you see that?" Here we fucking go "Mushrooms kicking in then Lisa? What are you seeing now?" She was pointing her finger down towards her knee, trying to touch something, fuck's sake. "Can you see that? Can you see the chewing gum? It's all coming up from the floor, it's floating." I wasn't pissed enough for this shit, but I couldn't help but piss myself laughing, then the other two fuckers started. "Yeah, I can see it too, but I can't touch it, why can't I touch it?" I needed to get these fuckers back to the hotel ASAP, I just had visions of all three going absolutely AWOL and me chasing them all over fucking Amsterdam. "Girls, are you hungry?" I thought food may tempt them, expecting them to have a case of the munchies. "Yeah, I'm fucking starving, please feed me, feed me now, I'm soooooo hungry." Cara begged. I was onto a winner here, "Right ok girls let's go get a load of munchies and go back to the room and eat like absolute fucking pigs."

Thankfully after all the hallucinations that followed the chewing gum, I got them safely back to the hotel room. They all ate their weight in crisps and chocolate and all three passed out and were snoring their heads off. Once I took a cheeky video, because that is what they would and have done to me in the past, I decided to go back out on my own, only down to the bar next to the hotel. That experience had sobered me up pretty quickly and be fucked was I going to bed at 4.30pm; I loved an early night, but not that bloody early. "Two shots of tequila and one beer please?" The bar was very quiet, but it was nice, I felt safe and didn't have far to crawl back to the hotel room. A few drinks in, I'd made a few friends and was starting to feel the effects of the alcohol again.

My new 'friends' left, and I was alone again, that was until the most unbelievable thing happened. I turned on my stool and caught a glimpse of someone walking into the bar, someone I recognised. He was tall, blonde hair, blue eyes, and the hottest fucking man on earth. It couldn't be? Not here, not now? What the actual fuck, it's Finn,

IT'S FINN FUCKING HOLSTON!!!!!!!!!!

Chapter 9

Finn Fucking Holston

I sat there just staring, doubting myself, had the girls

drugged me and slipped mushrooms into my drink?

Was I hallucinating? He was walking towards me

and I looked like an absolute gimp, opened-mouthed,

looking special. Snap out of it bitch, NOW! I

pulled myself together (not really, I just appeared

that way on the outside) swivelled round on my

chair, to act like I didn't care. I was cool, calm, and

collected. He came in and sat down at the bar, on

the stool right fucking next to me, fuck, fuck, fuck.

My heart was beating out of my chest and I felt like I

was having a panic attack. I can smell him, OMG I

can smell him, what is that? It smells like pure

fucking heaven, I wanted to jump on top of him right

now and straddle that fucker, fuck. Right pull it together now Sophie. Could I bring myself to even look at him? I know, I'll order another drink; I waved the bar tender down. "Beer please?" I said with a smile, "Make it two," He said in the most sexy, deep gruff voice. Fuck, fuck, fuckedy, fuck, fuck, fuck, he made my fanny twinge, he made me wet, I swear I just laid a fucking slug or ten in my pants! I turned and looked at him, and he was looking back at me with the most dazzling smile I'd ever seen, fuck he melted me. I wanted to be cool and act like I didn't know who he was, I just looked back at him and smiled, those eyes, I could get lost in them forever, he really was fucking perfect. "I'll get these." he said as he handed me my beer, "Hi, I'm Finn, what are you doing drinking all alone? Or is your husband in the toilet or something?" OMG now I would actually have to speak, how was I going to speak? "Thanks Finn, I'm Sophie and no husband. I'm here alone, long story, am here for a girl's weekend. They all decided to get fucked up on space cake and mushrooms, I got them back to the hotel room and decided to come back out and socialise." My god why was I so breathless? All I'd done was speak for a second and I couldn't fucking breathe. I couldn't stop looking into his eyes, every now and then I'd remember that I probably looked like a fucking psycho and would look away now and then. My body was deceiving me and doing things beyond my control, stop fucking betraying me body, please? He was looking back and smiling at me to be fair, and he did just buy me a drink, so maybe it wasn't all one-sided, unless he was just being nice? I had read somewhere about what a gentleman he was. "Well fuck me, that's a good way to break the ice" he said as he laughed. I didn't think it was that funny to be honest, though I was glad that what happened, happened as I was here now, with FUCKING FINN. "Well, I like to leave an impression, so we have established why I'm here alone, why are you here all alone, chatting to this crazy Welsh bird?" My voice had stopped shaking now and I was feeling a bit more at ease, still wanted to rip his fucking clothes off though, but my body wasn't betraying me as it was earlier and I'd loosened up. "I'm here for work, have been here a few days, I leave on Sunday. Have been coming in here most evenings as it's quite quiet. Crazy welsh bird eh? I'd never have guessed you were welsh, do I make a sharp exit now?" As he said that, he winked - he fucking winked at me. I think I just fucking laid another slug, I had the most fanny flutters I'd ever had. Fuck, he knew what he was doing, the grin on his face said it all, he was so fucking charismatic, I was sure he could have any woman he wanted.

Once I'd calmed the fuck back down, I finished my drink and ordered another fucker, I needed to be pissed to find my confidence. "Yes, I'd run now, get out whilst you still can! Before I take you home and tie you up in my dungeon." What the fuck was coming out of my mouth? As I said it, I turned bright red and felt like an absolute twat! Why did I always put my foot in my mouth whenever I was around someone remotely attractive? "Hmmmmm, thing is I think I would like that, a lot." Jesus what do I say to that "Well play your cards right Finn and you never know what could happen." I winked back but it didn't go according to plan as I looked like I'd had a stroke! He was pissing himself laughing, I couldn't be sexy if I tried. Fuck it, I'll laugh the prick into bed.

Countless drinks deep and many conversations later, I was fucking bolloxed. I'd told him all about me and now it was his turn. Truth was I couldn't concentrate - I was just looking, longingly into his eyes and nodding my head, wishing he would just kiss me already. He hadn't once mentioned his job, as in the fact he was quite a famous actor. I obviously knew this but hadn't said anything in case he wanted an escape, which it seemed he did. "And then I decided to go into acting, which I love, but what I don't enjoy is the attention, and constantly feeling like you're being watched. I just want a bit of normality when work is over, it is hard work looking over your shoulder all the time. This is why I've enjoyed it here; no one has recognised me yet, not even you!" Whoop there it is, guess I spoke too soon. "That's where you're wrong Mr Holston, I knew who you were as soon as you walked through the door, just figured you'd want a normal conversation, wasn't expecting you to even speak to me to be honest. It must be hard for you, no rest for the wicked, I guess. But at least there are still some places you can go to unwind and feel normal again. And I have to be honest, you're so much nicer than I was expecting. I know you shouldn't judge a book by its cover but, someone that looks the way you do, that can have anyone or anything they want, you would expect a hint of arrogance, but I'll take my hat off to you, you're lovely."

At that moment he grabbed hold of me and gave me a hug, I felt electricity surging through every inch of my body. As we slowly pulled away from each other his cheek brushed mine, he grabbed my head and slowly eased his tongue in my mouth. In response I grabbed him back and moved my tongue against his, my heart felt like it was ripping through my chest, this was the best kiss I'd ever experienced, and it wasn't just because he was famous. I felt something - I don't know what it was I hadn't felt it before, yes there was a longing and my pussy was tingling and wet but there was something else, something I couldn't describe, it was fucking perfect, he was fucking perfect.

Then my phone started vibrating, fucking girls were awake and ringing me, it was already 9pm so they'd been out for the count for a while, and I had been sat with Finn for a good few hours, didn't feel like that though. Where the fuck had the time gone? As we pulled away, he just looked and me and said, "Well fuck." I nodded and said, "Fuck indeed, I need to get this a sec, just to let the girls know I'm safe a minute."

Once I'd finally got them off the phone and reassured them I'd be home soon, I got back to Finn. I hadn't had time to process what had just happened. He kissed me, and it was the best kiss I'd ever experienced, and not just because I was pissed, wow, I had no other words. "All sorted, beautiful?" Fuck I wanted him so bad, was I dreaming? "Yes, all sorted, got them off my back for a bit, they do still sound a little worse for wear, so they won't be conducting a search party anytime soon." He looked at me and he looked sad, oh god, what's he going to say? That this was a mistake and we're from separate worlds, blah, blah, blah. God please not yet, I want more. "Sophie, I have had the best night, well the best night I've ever had. You really are an amazing woman, inside and out, I really want to get to know you more and spend some time with you. But I do have to go soon, I have to be up for work at 3am and I need some sleep. I don't want to leave you though; can I have your number? I really want to see you again." I thought this was coming, he's fobbing me off now, he's kissed me in a moment of madness and now he's thinking fuck and backtracking and using work as an excuse to escape. "Listen Finn, there's no pressure, I've had an amazing time getting to know you, and I enjoyed that kiss even more, but if you are regretting it now you don't need to make excuses, it's fine I get it."

Before I'd finished my sentence, he grabbed me and kissed me again, this time we weren't interrupted. If this was all that was going to happen then I was still grateful, but I can't imagine not feeling his hands or mouth on me ever again, the thought made me want to cry. We'd only known each other for a few hours, and hadn't even slept together, but already I felt this attachment to him. I had to have him, now I had got to know a small part of him, I didn't ever want to be without him. I felt like I was going to cry, GET A FUCKING GRIP! As we pulled away again, he grabbed my face and looked me dead in the eye and said "Sophie, you're the most beautiful person I've ever had the pleasure of meeting, and I want to see you again, please can I have your number? Are you here tomorrow? If you are, we could meet here again tomorrow same time around 5ish?" Well fuck that felt sincere, maybe he meant it. "Give me your phone then?" I added my number, took a selfie of us both and saved it to my number in his phone. "Come on then Miss Rush, I'll walk you back to your hotel and then I'll go back to mine and we can see each other tomorrow." I got down off my stool and nearly went ass over tit. Luckily, he caught me, but I nearly took him out, he's very tall and skinny and I'm a chunky girl, bet he put his fucking back out catching hold of me, poor fucker, he seemed ok though.

At the entrance to the hotel, we kissed and hugged each other good night, and went our separate ways. I couldn't stop looking at him as he was walking away from me. "Don't forget, same time tomorrow Sophie!" he shouted back at me as he walked away. And yet I was still so scared that would be the last time I would ever lay eyes upon him. Fuck was that all a dream? I fucking hope not, it's been the best day of my entire life. I wonder if he will text tonight. I really hope so, I miss him already, could this really be happening? What did he see in me? This man looked like a fucking god and could undoubtedly have any woman he wanted, why would he like me, I just don't get it. Maybe it was just a bit of easy fun for him to keep him occupied whilst he was here in Amsterdam.

"Here she is!" Lisa shouted as I entered the room and they were all cheering. "So, where the fuck have you been then? We were worried, you've been gone ages." I sat down on the bed looking totally and utterly shell shocked. Cara grabbed me and said "What's the matter, you look like you're going to cry, what's wrong? Has someone hurt you?" I shook my head and held back the tears, finally I composed myself. "Girls make yourself comfortable, you're never going to believe what I am about to tell you."

Chapter 10

Was it all a dream?

I was rudely awoken by my alarm at 7am, I didn't want to wake up. I'd spent the whole night dreaming about Finn, it was lush, I kept dreaming about fucking him, I just hoped I would get to see him again. Yes, I wanted to fuck him so badly, but this felt more than just a physical attraction, this was so much more than that. Now I'd met him, I couldn't imagine my life without him; just the thought of never touching or kissing him again or even looking into those eyes again cut me deep already and I'd only known him one day. Anyway, enough of that negativity for one day, positive vibes only Sophie. I had a hell of a lot to be grateful for, especially the fact I had literally met the man of my dreams last night. I had spent an amazing few hours with him, and he actually wanted me too, he kissed me, he made the first move. Still had to pinch myself and was in total and utter disbelief about the whole thing. I think Cara, Kelly and Lisa thought I had lost the plot when I was telling them last night. You could see they didn't believe a word I was saying either, I would show the fuckers later on when I meet up with him tonight. God I can't wait to see his beautiful face again, I have a severe case of butterflies just at the thought of him right now.

"Right, come on you bunch of drug mules, time to get up and go do some sightseeing." Thought I'd wake the lazy fucktards up, wonder if I will get the strange looks again today. Wish I'd have taken that picture on my phone of me and Finn as proof, fuck that's a thought, I wonder if I've heard off him? As

I grabbed my phone off the side and checked for notifications there was nothing from Finn. I felt a major pang of disappointment, I know it's stupid, but I honestly felt like crying. Had he forgotten about me? Was he just pissed last night and was regretting everything this morning? My god I felt sick to my stomach, I needed to take my mind off the whole thing and just have a good day with the girls. Maybe he just wasn't much of a texter, I just don't understand men one bit, if I'd have got his number, I would've definitely text him and looked desperate by now. So it's probably a good thing I don't have his number, I can play it cool, even though I have no choice it gives the appearance that I am chilled about the whole thing. Maybe he doesn't want to text yet as he will appear too eager and put me off? God I hate all these stupid games, and I hate dating and how vulnerable it makes me feel.

First, we went on a canal cruise, which was nice and relaxing, though the girls all had sore heads so didn't particularly seem to enjoy it. We took lots of selfies though; we were all filtered right up as none of us particularly looked great today. As we were cruising down the canal, I caught site of what looked like a film set and then I caught a glimpse of that perfect fucking back of Finn's. "Sophie what are you looking at? Ooooo is that him FINN, FINN, WHERE FOR ART THOU FINN!" OMG I was going to kill Cara if she didn't shut the fuck up right now. I'd never moved so quickly before in my life; I tripped over someone's foot and nearly fell off the side of the fucking boat. I grabbed hold of her and put my hands over her massive gob "SHUT THE

FUCK UP!". She fucking bit my hand because I had
her gripped so tightly she couldn't breathe, my god
we can't even behave on a little boat trip. Thank
fuck he didn't hear her, everyone on the boat found
it highly fucking hysterical, but I was bright red and
less than impressed, twats!

I'd never been so glad to get off a fucking boat in my
life "Come on Sophie, don't be grumpy I was only
messing." Cara grabbed me. "I know dick head,
you just live to embarrass me, where next bitch?" I
was dreading this answer, I wanted to see so much
whilst we were here, just hoped I could take my
mind off Finn and actually soak in all the culture.
"Anne Frank's house is next." Brilliant, this is
something I'd always wanted to see, and I knew this
would keep me occupied for a while and hopefully

take my mind off the fact I'd not heard a peep from Finn all day!

After a few hours of exploring Amsterdam and taking in its wonderful history and culture, we got back to the hotel, so we could shower and get ready for the evening out. By this time, I was really starting to feel anxious about seeing Finn, that is if he was even going to show up. It was 3pm and I'd still not heard anything from him whatsoever. Yes, I understood he was busy working, but surely he took breaks right? My god, I was never this needy, I just really wanted to hear something from him. I just want some reassurance that he A) remembers what happened with us last night and B) doesn't bloody regret it. I guess I would be put out of my misery soon, one way or another. I don't know what I will do if he doesn't show up, I will look like I have made it all up for a start and my mates will think I am even more crazy than they already do! More importantly I would be absolutely devasted. He already meant a lot to me and I couldn't explain it in my own head. I needed to get a grip and I needed to do it quickly.

I gave myself a good talking to, showered and put my big girl pants on and had a few drinks to unwind a little bit, which was working for five minutes until everyone started taunting me again. "Can't wait to meet your fella later Sophie" Lisa gave a wink as the words left her mouth. "Yeah, that's if he's not imaginary and it's all Sophie being completely delusional" Cheers Cara. "Fuck off all of you, I won't go at all you all keep on, I've not heard off him all day so knowing my shit luck with men he won't turn up. I feel anxious enough without you lot winding me up, I don't even want to go now". Everyone stayed quiet for a minute before they burst out laughing and told me to get a grip. They reassured me they wouldn't think I was crazy and whatever happened, we would have a good time.

As we arrived back at the bar where I had met Finn - late may I add, thanks to Cara - I had a quick look around and couldn't see him anywhere. My heart literally sank, and I had a horrible feeling in the pit of my stomach: where the fuck was he? Maybe he was just running late, was held up with filming. I guess it wasn't just a clocking off time with his job and you just had to keep working until you got it right. "Time for shots" I said to the girls as I was acting like I wasn't anxious as hell about Finn not being here.

We rapidly got very pissed and had attracted a group of men to our table, where we were playing a host of drinking games, which only added to our drunken state. It was 8pm now, three hours after Finn was meant to show up. I'd actually given up now and had accepted Finn really was making a sharp exit last night – what a wanker! Can't say I blame him, not as if he could take me to red carpet appearances, the journalists would be asking why Shamu was on his arm and not in the fucking sea. I genuinely thought there was a connection, but we had both had a lot to drink and I was always going to want him more than he wanted me, I mean, look at him. I wanted to hate him, but I couldn't. Gutted was the understatement of the century and I just wanted to go home and wallow in self-pity.

Then everything went blank, I don't remember any fucking thing!

Chapter 11

Fuck my life

As I woke from my slumber, I found that not only did I have dribble all up the side of my face yet again, but I was also bollock naked, and there was a man, also bollock naked led next to me. As I led there totally still, so as not to wake up the gentleman friend led next to me, I hoped the dribble on my face was that and not his semen, and I tried to rack my stupid brain as to what the fuck had happened last night. Who was led next to me? Pretty sure it wasn't Finn as he never fucking showed up, prick. Whoever it was, couldn't have been great in bed as I can't bloody remember, nor did I feel like anyone had been down there! I really wanted to turn and look but was scared, please be hot? Please be hot? I couldn't cope with waking up to an absolute minger, not after everything that had happened this weekend, the girls would never let me live it down.

As I lay there praying for a miracle, he turned to face me and I felt his hard cock on my side. "Good Morning beautiful." He said in a foreign accent. It was too early for me to work out where he was from and I was way too hungover. God, I felt so fucking sick and wanted to scream 'get your fucking cock off me you pig.' I managed to contain my anger as I turned my head to see what the damage was. Hmmm, he could've given pig man a run for his money, put it that way, and now I could feel the precum leaking off his cock onto my side, it took all my might not to heave and throw up all over the dirty bastard.

I shot out of bed and ran to the bathroom, where I threw up a good few times, before I mustered the strength to get into the shower and wash my fucking disgusting sins away. I seriously had fucking issues, how quickly life could change! Friday I met and kissed Finn fucking Holston and yesterday I got stood up, got wankered and took a right cracker to bed. How was I going to get out of this now? I bet he was one of these that you couldn't get rid of, for fuck's sake Sophie.

I shit my fucking pants (if I was wearing any) as there was a loud bang on the door "Come back to bed miss beautiful, I will look after you." YUCK!!!! He made my fucking skin crawl. Enough is enough, I'm going to have to get out and be a big girl and tell him to leave. After I recovered from the mini heart attack, I pulled myself together and left the safe zone of the bathroom, still looking rather dishevelled. I gave a little smile to my guest on the bed. "Hey, sorry I wasn't feeling well, too much alcohol last night. Speaking of, I am really sorry, but I can't remember a thing from last night and I definitely don't remember you coming back here with me, no offence." I was cringing as I said it, why did I do this to myself, I am a first-class KNOB. "Did we? I mean did we do anything sexual?" Oh my god I sounded like a total bitch. "Sophie, I can't believe we had the most incredible night together and you can't remember anything, it was the best night of my life." Fucking wonderful, now I look like a total bitch. "Do you even remember my name?" Fucking hell, he's not going to make this easy, he looked genuinely sad. "I…. I have to be honest, no I don't I'm sorry, I'm not intentionally being mean, but I don't remember any details of the evening past around 8pm." He looked up at me and burst out laughing. I was taken aback for a moment or two, what was going on? "Sophie, I'm joking with you. Firstly, my name is Miguel and you were all over me in the pub, you begged me to come back for a cwtch, whatever the hell that is, we kissed, took our clothes off and got into bed, you fell asleep." I don't think I ever felt so relieved in my whole, entire life! He was still laughing; thank god he had a sense of humour or this would be even more awkward than it already was. "Oh, thank god, Miguel I am so sorry. A cwtch is a cuddle or hug, it's something Welsh people say. Please don't hate me, I was very drunk and blacked out." Mid-sentence, Cara banged the shit out of the door and shouted, "Come on we have a plane to catch!" Ah perfect timing, hopefully he will bugger off now and I can get to the part where my mates take the piss out of me all day. "And that's my cue to leave, it was a pleasure to meet you Sophie, any chance of your number so we can stay in touch?" Oh, my Christ, no! I'm going to have to give him the wrong number just so I can get him out of here and avoid further embarrassment. "Yeah sure, I won't reply for a while as I'll be in the air, pass me your phone and I'll stick the number in for you. Even though I can't remember anything, it's been nice to meet you." I put my number in his phone and gave him a friendly hug "Sophie, I really like you, have a safe trip and I'll hopefully see you again soon." Fucking doubt that mate, I thought as he left and breathed a massive sigh of relief, thank fuck that was over!

That drama over, we were on route to the airport, I'd already had the piss taken out of me since I had surfaced from the hotel room. Now the videos were coming out, they always seemed to catch me acting a twat when I was pissed, and always had videos for evidence, they loved nothing more than showing me the next day and making me feel more embarrassed than I already did. Christ, I was definitely pissed, and definitely all over Miguel and most other people that were in the bar last night! I shouldn't be let out, I was a fucking liability. I blame Finn standing me up, I would never have got that pissed if he was there. "Oh, we're here, what a shame, no time to look at any more videos, I seem to remember having a video of you fuckers from Friday aswell, so don't even think about posting that on social media or I will too, you're not the only ones to take videos this weekend mind."

As we took off, we were all looking a much rougher version of the individuals that had arrived on Friday. We'd all had an amazing time and had some memorable experiences and a good bit of girly bonding time. Couldn't wait to get back home to my girls now and tell them all about the crazy weekend, (I would leave out the Finn and Miguel bits though). I'd come to the conclusion, that few hours with Finn were all I was ever going to get and to take it for what it was, fun. When I get back I was going to focus on myself and my kids and that was it, no men, they can all piss the fuck off!

Chapter 12

Me, Myself and I, hold that thought

Thank fuck I booked today off! I thought to myself as Monday morning began. The kids were in an absolutely joyful mood this morning which was lovely. Marie was screaming at Emily because she was taking too long in the bathroom, and because Marie was screaming at her, Emily was taking even longer just to piss her off. "Happy families" I sang to my beautiful children as I tried to stop them ripping each other's faces off. "Girls come on now, be nice, I know you hate mornings, especially Monday mornings, but we're all in the same boat. We all have to get up and go to school and work." I of course didn't have to as I'd booked the day off but fuck was I going to tell them, they would kick right off if they knew I was on leave today.

Once I'd done the school run and had dropped off my little cherubs, I went and got a massive McDonalds breakfast. I was so fucking hungry, I was eating like a right scruffy bitch, thank fuck no one could see me right now! My plans for the day were to mostly chill, have my nails done and just process everything that had happened over the last few weeks - it had been quite out of the ordinary, even for me. At least now I wouldn't have to be going on dates in order to get a ticket to meet Finn, as I'd already met the fucker, kissed him and lost him all in the space of a day. I could relax knowing I wouldn't have to be anywhere or see anyone I didn't want to. I was done with men, they could all go and fuck themselves, in the ass, dry, literally. If a nice one came along now and then, then I might chuck him a fuck, if he was a bit of alright like, but I am done falling for anyone or catching feelings of any sort, feelings can fuck right off! At this point I had come to the realisation, I was destined to be alone forever, and I was ok with that. No lying awake at night worrying if my man is out cheating on me, or finally meeting the most amazing guy and finding out he is already taken, or even better, meeting the man of your dreams and he stands you up and doesn't fucking contact you, adios mother fuckers and good riddance!

Hold that thought! I almost had a mini heart attack when some fucker pounded on my door, that was a police knock if ever I'd heard one. As I got to the door, I had a massive sinking feeling, like my guts were falling out of my asshole. Fuck's sake, it was

Caleb, here we go again, I was not falling for any shit he needed to fucking leave and right now. "What the fuck are you doing here Caleb, I told you I never wanted to see you again, you've ripped my heart and fucking trampled on it for the last time, now fuck off." With that I slammed the door in that fucker's face, ha my god I felt like a badass bitch, I did it! I finally didn't succumb to his charm or his bullshit. To be fair, I didn't let him speak which was good thinking on my part. "Sophie, please answer the door, I'm not leaving until you open this door, I have something to tell you and it's important, I promise I am not here to upset you." Fuck, what the fuck does that mean? God don't fall for it Sophie, this is how he reels you in. "I'm not falling for your shit Caleb, you will have a long fucking wait out there in the cold, so I hope you enjoy freezing your cock off, you prick." I couldn't help but feel a pang

of guilt at the thought of him freezing his lovely

cock off. "Sophie please answer this fucking door,

I've left her, I want to be with you, no more messing

around this time. I want you; I've only ever wanted

you, please?" Holy fuck was he for real? This was

all I wanted to hear for a very long time, and now

he'd said it, I felt a state of panic, what the fuck was

that all about? I stood there in a state of shock for a

few seconds, then I decided to open the door before

all the neighbours came out to watch the show.

There he was, looking rather upset with his bags and

some flowers, uh did he think he was moving in here

or what? Cheeky prick. "Come in, you have five

minutes, I have somewhere I need to be, so don't get

too comfortable." My god I was savage today! As I

said it, I looked at his bags as if to hint that there was

no way he was fucking moving in here with me.

"Don't worry, I'm not expecting to move in, I had to come here on my way to my mates, I'm going to stay with him for a bit until I get my own place sorted. I just had to come see you, I've missed you so much. After you threw me out last week, I had to take action, I can't be without you any longer. I've told her I don't want to be with her anymore a few days ago and have moved out today. I'm going to get my own place, but that is going to take a few weeks. I know I have a lot to prove, and I need to make things up to you, but please give me another chance. I will beg if I have to Soph. I want you and only you, forever."

My god he seemed pretty serious! Again, I was in total and utter shock, I'd waited so long to hear this and for him to actually prove it, now it was happening I was speechless, and being totally honest, wasn't sure if this was even what I wanted anymore. Don't get me wrong, I still looked at him and wanted to fuck the shit out of him, but I think he had just hurt me so many times that I was kind of over it now. It was either that or it was my way of protecting myself from being hurt again. Caleb grabbed my head "Look at me Sophie, I love you and I want you; please can we try, we can go at whatever pace you want, I just can't lose you." As I looked into his eyes, he melted me, as he always did. I loved him too I always would, but something didn't feel right, I had a nagging feeling, and I didn't know what it was. "Caleb, stop just let me think, I can't breathe, never mind think when you grab me like that. Listen, you've royally fucked me over for a very long time, how am supposed to believe a word that comes out of your mouth? How do I know she's not ended things with you, and you thought, 'I know, I'll run back to Sophie that stupid bitch will take me back'? I can't trust you, so how will we ever work?"

As I pushed him away, he burst into tears. Oh, wow now I felt bad and surely, he couldn't fake tears. It was normally me crying over him, oh how the tables had turned, 'suffer' I thought to myself, before I reverted back to feeling bad and gave him a hug. Fuck, and if I did, I got that tingling feeling deep inside my pussy, it was just telling me to jump on his cock and ride fuck out of him. Oh my god, why did this always happen to me? My head is strong, and my pussy lets me down, every god damn time, fuck you vagina you traitorous bitch! You're supposed to be on my side, why do you have to be so greedy? He smelt out of this world, he had my favourite aftershave on, bastard did that on purpose to lure me in! Well, it wouldn't work this time, I was going to be strong, at least that's what I was telling myself, whilst getting incredibly wet. My pussy, the betrayer, was liking this too much, I had to pull away before I did something I would regret later. As I did, he grabbed my face and said, "I love you Sophie, only you, please just give me a chance?" He went in for the kiss and I couldn't resist any fucking longer; I straddled him and grabbed his head and kissed him back passionately. I felt his cock get hard against my pussy and I began to rub against it as we kissed. I was aching for him; I just wanted to feel his nice, big, hard cock inside me, right fucking NOW. I'd fully given in to him as he pushed me onto the floor to take off my leggings and my soaking knickers. He kissed and licked my inner thighs, "I love you

Sophie, and I love your pussy". He teased me for ages, kissing and licking my inner thighs. Every time he got close to my pussy he would stop and say "Do you want me? Tell me you want me to taste you." I was so fucking horny by this point; I was sure if he touched me I would cum instantly. I slid two of my fingers inside myself and let out a little moan of pleasure as I did. When I took them out, I put them in his mouth and said, "I want you to taste me Caleb, I want you." With that he started licking my clit and sliding his tongue inside me, fuck it was good, he was a sexy bastard. My mind started to wander and I imagined it was Finn between my legs, licking every inch of my pussy, FUCK I felt the pressure intensifying and I moaned like fuck as I gave into the pleasure. Oh my god I needed to not fantasize about Finn right now, it had totally thrown me off. I needed to get back into it with CALEB.

He slid his tongue up the length of my body to my

nipples and neck, then rubbed his hard cock on my

soaking wet clit and teased my pussy by sliding it in

a little bit and taking it back out. "I want to feel you

inside me Caleb" and with that he slid his rock-hard

cock inside me, grabbed my hair and kissed me. I

dug my nails into his back, and we fucked; good, old

fashioned, rough hard sex. I bit his neck as I came

again, and he gave in and he came deep inside me.

Fuck I felt thoroughly fucked, so much so my legs

were shaking and felt like jelly. We both led there in

silence, catching our breath for a few minutes, before

he turned to me and said, "So is that a yes then?" I

just gave him the death glare, "so you think because

we fucked it's a yes?" He looked as if he'd shit his

pants. "Caleb, we can try dating and see where it

goes, but I am not promising anything, and we take it at a snail's pace, these are my terms, if you don't like it there is no room for negotiation." He was over the moon and grabbed me and kept thanking me, so I kissed him to shut him up, and the inevitable happened again and again until I realised I had to leave to have my nails done. I sent him on his way and left to have a pamper session, though I was struggling to walk properly.

For the whole time I sat there, I was trying to process what had happened, these last few weeks had been a total and utter head fuck. I couldn't work out why I didn't feel over the moon with what had transpired today. If that had been a few months ago I would've been really happy and excited, and straight on the phone to the girls to tell them every last detail. But right now, I felt like I had done something wrong; it didn't make sense, this was the one time I hadn't done anything wrong. "You ok Sophie? You've been really quiet today, it's not like you." Oh god, I was sitting here racking my brains, looking like a right ignorant bitch, so I filled her in on everything that had happened. "Christ Sophie, you don't do things by half do you!" No, I fucking didn't, I was a pain in the arse, but it was me. I was a magnet for stupid shit and weird situations.

Once my nails were done, I went to pick my darling children up and went home for the evening - wine was needed this evening and a copious amount at that! As me, Emily and Marie sat watching some romantic comedy I can't remember the name of, I was balls deep into the bottle of wine, so much so I had to open a second and I sat wondering what had happened to Finn again, it was bugging the shit out of me. I just wanted answers either way, did he regret meeting me? Or was it just a case of he was so pissed he couldn't remember. I needed to move on from all of that though, it was something I would never have closure for, not only that I had agreed to give things a go with Caleb. Now this is something I should be overjoyed with, but I still have that niggling feeling. I couldn't tell the kids yet either because they know how much he hurt me, they wouldn't be best pleased. They would make him pay for him hurting me and it was going to be awkward as hell, so would Cara, Lisa and Kelly, maybe that's why I was not excited because of all the shit that comes with being with Caleb.

If we were really meant to be though, we would get through it, one way or another. I decided to tell everyone tomorrow, that we're taking it slow and to see what happens, no promises; I just wanted to

enjoy tonight without anyone knowing and being on

my case.

Chapter 13

Getting the ick

As the weeks went on and everything was out in the open, it was clear to me that something was missing. It wasn't a lack of love, or chemistry or anything I could put my finger on, there was just something that wasn't quite right. It was as if he had stopped trying, which pissed me off as I wanted spontaneity and effort, I wanted to be whisked away for a weekend now and again. I booked a hotel myself, for us both just to get away together and all he did was fucking complain because the football was on. This was not how I had pictured my life going at all, but we sat down and I warned him I was at the end of my tether, he agreed to buck his ideas up, so I gave him the chance to do just that.

And then the pandemic hit, and everything really went to shit; due to restrictions put in place we had to form bubbles, so Caleb came to stay with us. Things were not going great, which was the understatement of the century. We argued almost daily, and I wanted to happy-slap his face with a chair just at the sight of him. I felt so guilty for feeling like this, but I just couldn't seem to shake it off. What made it worse was the fact I couldn't even go anywhere to get away from him, not even work as everyone was made to work from home. I did have an enormous amount of love for him, but I was officially getting the ick and needed a break.

Thankfully I didn't have to wait long until we were out of lockdown again; granted we couldn't go about our normal business, but we could leave the house and meet up with people, provided we wore masks and took relevant precautions. It was surreal meeting up in the pub with restricted numbers, but I didn't care I needed a night out with the girls, they would help me sort my head out. "There she is, I've missed you so much." With that I burst into tears, in bloody public, this had been building up for so long I wasn't at all surprised. "Oh my god, we're not that bad, are we?" I could tell by Lisa, Kelly and Cara's faces that they just wanted to grab hold of me and hug me. I was glad in a way we had to stay socially distanced, because if I had a hug, I don't think I'd stop crying. I finally pulled myself together and downed the glass of wine that the girls had so kindly pre ordered for me. "Girls my head is proper fucked, things with me and Caleb aren't good at all. I was reluctant to give us a chance when he turned up at the house and I wish I'd trusted my gut and said no. Don't get me wrong I love him to bits, but there is just something missing; we've arguing quite a bit since we've been in lockdown. Arguing is normal I get that, but not all the bloody time. We were sorting the garden out the other day and he started, and I honestly wanted to smash a paving slab over his skull. That's not me, it's not who I am, I love him but I fucking hate him at the same time. I still think about Finn all the time, especially when we're having sex, I know we all fantasize but is that normal all the time? Do I just have unrealistic expectations, and this is actually what 'being happy' is like? Because if it is, I'm not sure I want it, I was happier on my own to be honest. I need another drink; I'll leave you all to ponder that information whilst I get another round in."

I ordered two drinks, I needed it to unwind, I was wound up like a fucking top. "Jesus, Sophie's on a mission" Kelly piped up as I walked back over. "She needs it after holding all of that in for so long, give the girl a break." Lisa had my back. "Yeah, what she said, so come on then hit me with it girls, I can see you're all dying to tell me what you think." I reached for my glass and eagerly awaited their take on things. "I'll go first." I knew Cara would be first to jump in, bless her. "So, here's my take on things, you love to live in a fantasy land you always have, no offence, that's just who you are. All relationships are hard work Soph, they are never straight forward and plain sailing. I honestly think you had just built up this fantasy in your mind, like something you've seen on a film and expect it to be amazing 100% of the time, life isn't like that. You need to get a grip on reality, if you truly love him like you have said you do then you need to snap out of this. Yes, you met Finn, and being brutally honest he never contacted you again, so as far as you should be concerned that is done, you need to draw a line under Finn. Sorry if that is harsh but this is the real world we're living in. If the love has gone and you don't feel anything for him anymore then fair enough, knock things on the head, but if you love him you need to work at it. Do you really think all of these stupid fuckers gushing all over social media are as happy as they make out on there? No, it's all a bloody show, behind closed doors they are going through just as much shit as everyone else, it's not all happiness and rainbows all the time." Well fuck, she was brutal, but I loved her honesty, and at least I'd got the worst one out of the way, the other two would be a lot nicer in their delivery.

"So as much as I agree with Cara, I got to say you really don't sound happy at all. Everyone has ups and downs, yes, but are you having more downs at the moment? That's what you need to ask yourself. You also need to ask yourself if you are self-sabotaging this relationship. Caleb hurt you, multiple times may I add, and I can't help but wonder if this is your way of protecting yourself from him hurting you again? Or is there really something missing and you realise that because when you met Finn it was different, even if it was only for a few hours? Have you actually spoken to Caleb and told him how you feel? Maybe it's worth you both having a few days of space to sort your head out." Kelly made a lot of sense and as expected wasn't so brutal, she already made me feel a little better, maybe space was what I needed.

"Save the best until last. I think it's not right, if your gut is telling you there is something missing then there is. I'm not just saying that because I don't like him after everything he has put you through in the past, you should always trust your gut, it's never failed you yet. I think you should sit him down as Kelly said, tell him that you need a bit of space, and then I think me and you should go up to London for Comicon to go see Finn, you can get the closure you need then." Oh, wow that piqued my interest, seeing Finn? Not sure this sounded like a good plan, but I definitely wanted to, but would I look stupid going all the way up there to go see him?

"Thanks guys, I really appreciate the honesty, no matter how brutal Cara was. Lisa and Kelly, you are both right, I definitely need to sit down with him and tell him I am feeling a bit claustrophobic and suggest we have a few days apart. That's the problem. I can't even think straight because I have no me time, I can't even escape to work. I am so used to being on my own and doing my own thing, this is just totally alien to me now and it makes me anxious. With regards to Finn, we can't go to Comicon, we don't have tickets remember? It's sold out now and I didn't hold up my end of the bargain as everything went to shit. Not only that I am going to look like a fucking stalker paying £250 just to meet someone that fucking stood me up." Even though it made me a stalker I wanted to see him, just for an explanation, not that I would get one, but I fucking deserved one!

"The part about us not having tickets isn't strictly true." Lisa pulled two tickets out of her bag and waved them in the air. "We bought these when we made the bet with you, we didn't really care about you going on a date every day. All we wanted was to get you to put yourself out there and be wined and dined a bit, if you were 69'd as well that would've been a bonus. That night you said about it we saw how much you wanted to go, so we decided to get the tickets then. I only have an entrance ticket to the con, whereas you have the meet and greet experience. You won't be able to touch him as there will be a plastic screen between you, which at this point could be a good thing, given how angry you are at the moment. But you will be able to talk to him for a few minutes, you also get a photo with him. I've booked the train tickets, we will go up early morning and come back later on the same night. It's this Saturday if you're still up for it?"

Oh god I had butterflies just thinking about seeing him again. I'd felt so down for so long, I was actually smiling from ear to ear for the first time in ages. "Fuck it, let's do this shit, but don't let me make a complete twat of myself, no alcohol before I see him." Now my mind was fucking racing, what was I going to wear? What would he be like? Would he even remember me? I felt so happy and excited, I can't remember much after the next few drinks.

I can remember being at home though and jumping on Caleb telling him I love him, wanting to have sex and then falling asleep, that went down like a sack of shit as you can imagine. My plan was to come home and tell him I wanted space; instead I got absolutely wankered and told him I loved him, tried it on, then fell asleep. I really didn't help myself; I was a total and utter knob jockey!

Chapter 14

Thank fuck for that

When my alarm went off, I actually wanted to launch my phone through the fucking window, it felt like my head was in a vice and I would've cried if it wouldn't have made it more painful. "Fuck my actual life, why did I get so smashed last night?" I said to Caleb as he was spooning me with his cock digging in my ass. I wanted to make it clear I was in no mood for that this morning. He didn't take the hint though "I know what will make you feel better, shall we finish where we left off last night beautiful?" Nooooooooooo I wanted to cry right now; I love sex but not when I felt like I was actually going to die. Plus, I had to tell him I wanted a bit of space, if I fuck him and then effectively chuck him (that's how he will see it) he won't be happy.

"Babes we need to talk, sorry to dampen the mood, but I really need to get some stuff off my chest." I felt him sigh, which pissed me off, we clearly had issues and he was more fucked off he couldn't get his dick wet. "Listen, I love you but we're really not working at the moment, we're arguing all the bloody time and I think it's because we have spent every waking moment together. We need to sort this out now or this is only going one way. I know I am a nightmare to live with because I have been on my own for so long, but it's no walk in the park living with you either. I think maybe we need a little bit of space, maybe a few days away from each other where you stay at yours maybe, what do you think?" I felt like I spoke about a million miles an hour as I said it, but I just had so much going on in my brain I needed to get it out before I fucked up what I was trying to say.

"I knew this was coming, you're trying to push me away, you have been from the start, I'm not going anywhere this time Sophie no matter how hard this is, we're meant to be together, and I will fight for this. I won't let you push me away; we have been arguing a lot, yes, and we probably have spent too much time together. None of us have been going out to work so it has been unusual circumstances, but we can work through this I promise you. If you want a few days' space, I'll go back to the flat for a few days." Fucking hell, I wasn't trying to push him away I just needed to feel me again.

"Thanks for understanding babes, I'm not trying to push you away at all, I think this has just forced us into moving a lot quicker than what we would've had we not been locked down. I love you to pieces you know that, I just feel like you have given up making the effort now, in the beginning you would do nice things for me, like taking me away or running me a bath, cooking tea even. I feel like that has all gone out the window and all the effort is coming from my side which pisses me off and makes me an argumentative fucker then. I don't want to piss you off or be a bitch, I'm just being honest. And I know I am far from perfect, in fact I am a total fucking nightmare, so we both need to make an effort to make things better. I really think a bit of space will do us the world of good." With that we gave each other a kiss, and he managed to get his dick wet.

As I stood in the shower, I felt like a weight had been lifted, as awkward as that was, it needed to happen. And truth be told I couldn't wait to have some me time again, and more importantly, the bed to myself. Caleb was packing his stuff, he wasn't overjoyed about this, but he must know deep down it's for the best, we had to take some form of action, or it would end like all of my other relationships, in disaster. And neither of us wanted that, I was glad that was all off my chest and I wouldn't have to spend the day feeling guilty. Though I was looking forward to going up to London to see Finn, Caleb knew nothing about this, nor did he know what happened in Amsterdam; if he did, he would have a shit fit.

"Right, I'm all packed up and ready to go, how do you want to play this Sophie? Are we still going to see each other and speak, or do you want a complete break? Obviously, I don't want a complete break but will go with whatever you want to do." Oh god I thought I'd made it clear earlier. "I think we shouldn't see each other until next week now, I am in London tomorrow anyway. I still want to talk to you, we can ring and text, but just go back to how we were before lockdown, where we would see each other three to four times a week, what do you think?" Caleb nodded "yeah that sounds fair, just know I won't give up on you, I just really hope you can stop pushing me away and we can move past this."

What Caleb said made me feel really guilty, was this me pushing him away? Was I just being a total bitch with unrealistic expectations, maybe all these failed relationships were because of me? I blame all the chick flicks I had ever watched for my unrealistic expectations in men and love in general. I was fantasizing about another man I'd spent two seconds with, when I had the man I wanted for years and years. We'd gone through a lot to get to this point, he was living with me and yet I still wasn't happy. The sooner this was resolved the better, because I hated feeling like this.

Once I had snapped out of it, I made my way to work, I had really missed everyone, so was looking forward to having a good catch up, even if it meant getting fuck all work done. Hopefully pig man wouldn't be lingering in the car park like a sex pest, and I could have a trauma free morning. As I pulled in it was as if all my birthdays and Christmases had come at once, there was no one in the carpark whatsoever, phew.

As I walked into the office, Matt was waiting with the biggest grin on his face ever. "You missed me?" he shook his head "fuck no, just being polite and making you feel welcome, of course I have, it's not the same talking over skype, I need to know what you've been up to." I think everyone has gone a bit stir crazy over this lockdown and just being able to see people, even colleagues was bloody amazing.

Lunchtime came and I met up with Mandy, she looked fucking fabulous still, she'd had hell of a glow up, ending things with that fucktard was the best thing she could've ever done. It did make me wonder if monogamy was healthy, didn't fucking seem like it was, certainly wasn't for me at the moment anyway. "Hey beautiful, right fill me in on everything with Caleb, I feel like I've not seen you in decades." Oh god, I think we may need longer than the half an hour we were allowed for lunch for me to explain everything. I knew Mandy would be brutally honest too and wouldn't judge so I was happy to tell her everything like I had with the girls. "Well, where the fuck do I start, as you know we went to Amsterdam, it was a fantastic weekend to be fair, and I met Finn, you know all of that. Literally the day after I'd got back, I was having a chill and Caleb turned up at the door with his bags, he'd ended things with his ex and wanted to make a go of things with me. We talked and fucked a few times and I agreed to give it a go, but he wouldn't be moving in here, he'd need to get his own place, so we could take things slow and not rush into anything. At the time I did feel like even though I'd said yes, I maybe hadn't made the right decision, something just felt off. But I owed it to both of us to give it a go, as I love him and there is a lot of history, albeit tumultuous. It was going quite well for a few weeks, we were getting on well and enjoying being together, he was making the effort and taking me out, taking me away, everything I wanted basically. Then lockdown came and fucked everything up royally, we decided we'd rather see each other, even if it was all the time rather than never, so he moved in. From that point it was totally fucked, we both drove each other to the point of insanity, it's a miracle we haven't murdered each other. Aside from that, I can't stop thinking about Finn, even after what happened, I know I have to let it go, but there is just a niggling feeling I have, and I can't get him out of my head. Caleb thinks this is my way of protecting myself, and I am pushing him away to avoid myself getting hurt, but I really don't think that is what I am doing, unless I just don't know about it. Then last night me and the girls met up and they had the tickets for the Comicon on Saturday and said it would be a good idea to go and see him. I can talk to him, even just for a few minutes to get some closure on that night and what the bloody hell happened." I felt like I needed to come up for air after that.

"Christ, Sophie you don't do things by half do you! Like the time you wrote a letter to the Queen, requesting Henry VIII had a proper effigy and not just a slab in St George's chapel." Once she'd stopped pissing herself, she continued. "I think your friends are right in that seeing Finn tomorrow will be good to get some closure. I don't think this is your way of pushing Caleb away, I just think it's moved too quickly too soon. You need him to move back to his flat and go back to dating, who moves in with each other after a couple of weeks? That was always going to be a recipe for disaster, but I understand why you did it. Go tomorrow and see Finn, clear the air and leave that in the past, I mean it was never realistic anyway was it? Then come back and focus on what you want and whether Caleb is the right one for you." I'd had enough of going on about the same thing for ages, so felt a swift change of subject was in order.

"Anyway, that's enough of me and my endless dramas, what's going on with you? Any gossip? Have you been on dates?" As I said that she was beaming from ear to ear, which gave it away, there must've been someone in the picture. "Well since you ask, I have reconnected with someone from years ago, way before I was married, his name is Dylan, and he is just fucking phenomenal especially in the bedroom. We are taking things slow, but I honestly feel on cloud nine right now, he is amazing. I knew him from school and we always had a crush on each other, but it never went anywhere, I do feel like a giggly teenager again. I grin from ear to ear when he messages me, and he is just so thoughtful, he's always bringing me gifts and surprising me, couldn't be happier at the moment."

"Oh Mand, I am so happy for you, I really don't know anyone that deserves this more than you do. You'll be married twice, and I still wouldn't have had one wedding at this rate. We will have to go out on a double date somewhere soon, I need to meet him and vet him, check he is good enough for my work bestie." I looked at my watch and we'd been in the canteen for forty-five minutes. "We better get back, or the boss will sack us, even though we're the best staff on the planet and he would miss us too much."

Matt didn't sack us, thankfully and the rest of the afternoon absolutely flew by. I was glad to finish though and get home, where it would be just me and the kids, like old times. We decided to order a takeaway and watch a few films together, once I'd explained why Caleb wasn't here. They were glad of the break as well, they were used to it just being the three of us, and as much as we argued, they weren't used to it being constant like it was with Caleb. By 9pm I was in bed, star fishing - it was heaven, I wasn't missing Caleb but then I'd not had a chance to really. One thing was for certain, I wasn't missing him being in my bed, this was fucking lovely.

Chapter 15

Finn Holston, I'm coming for you

Saturday finally arrived, after spending the last few days trying to work out what I was going to say, what I was going to wear and how to do my makeup. Team that up with panicking at how he was going to react and if he would even remember me, was causing me major anxiety. As much as I was absolutely shitting my pants, I was also excited to see him again, even if it was just to get closure. Now to make myself look hot as fuck!

As I stood in the shower, I practiced my speech. "Well, hello you stupid knob face, enjoy standing me up did you? I'm not here because I care, I am here because my mates had already bought the tickets and didn't want to lose the money. I hope a thousand fleas infest your asshole and your arms are too short to fucking scratch it you wanker." Maybe that was a bit harsh, and contrary to me saying I didn't care, it really sounded like I did. Ok let's try a bit of honesty, maybe that'll come across a bit better. "Well, hello, I wanted to come today for some form of explanation as to why the hell you thought it was ok to lead me on and stand me up in Amsterdam? I've never been ghosted before and to be honest I can't get my head around it, why would you do that?" Nope that still didn't sound right, my god he was going to think I was mental, which I was - everyone is a little mental and if they aren't then they are boring. Right last time, "Hi Finn, hope your filming went well after I met you in Amsterdam.

Since I'd made that bet with the girls, they'd already got me the tickets, so here I am." Think that sounds cool, calm and collected and I didn't sound bothered that the prick had ghosted me. Of course, in reality, when I am face to face with him, it won't go that straightforward it never does. I still hadn't told Caleb, he knew I was going to London for the day, but thought I was Christmas shopping. I did feel guilty, but I wasn't doing anything, not as if I could hop on Finn's cock in front of thousands of people, well I could but I'd probably be arrested. I wasn't cheating I was just going to get closure so I could draw a line under what happened and move on with Caleb, without thinking about Finn all the time, and wondering what if?

I got out of the shower and started my makeup, whilst I sang my head off to some bad bitch music.

Had a perfect sassy mix of Beyonce, Arianna, Rhianna, I was feeling empowered and ready to take on the world and planned on looking hot whilst I did it. I imagined so many different scenarios about how this would go down, when he saw me. I imagined him calling security and calling me a crazy bitch. I had visions of him pushing the Perspex glass down, confessing his undying love for me, grabbing me and snogging my face off. Or him seeing me, turning and running for his life out of the room. To be fair the first and last options sounded the most likely, well I didn't have much longer to wait, shit I needed to stop daydreaming and get some clothes on, Lisa was picking me up to get the train in precisely 10 minutes. I'm normally ready hours too early, I hated having to rush ahhhhhh.

Thankfully I made it and was ready just in time, the kids didn't know I was going up to the Comicon, they thought I was Christmas shopping, so I had to make sure to bring some presents back later on. "Morning Soph, you look bloody lush fair play, you're going to make him regret what he did to you." Bless her I didn't quite believe her mind, the nerves were setting in now. "Lisa is this a stupid idea? I feel a bit sick now and I'm really not sure we should do this." Lisa shook her head "Oh no, you're not getting out of this, we're going, you need to do this no matter how awkward you feel right now, later you will be glad you did it, trust me. We're going to have a lovely day, spend a few hours on the train now with a couple of drinks for Dutch courage, bit of shopping, spot of lunch, go to the con for the meet and greet and then train back home." She was right,

I had to shut the fuck up, put my big girl pants on and get on with it.

As soon as we got on the train Lisa got the alcohol out ready, it was twelve o'clock, somewhere right? "Right, don't let me get wasted now and make a twat of myself". I said to Lisa as she popped the cork open on the champagne, yes cham fucking pagne. I would be smashed by 11am at this point, no doubt being sick and pissing all over this train but fuck it I needed something for the nerves. "I won't let you get in too much of a state Soph don't worry, it's just to take the edge off, we deserve it. Anyway, how are things with Caleb since you had the chat and he moved back out again? How did you find it last night being back to just the three of you again?" How did I say this without sounding like a bitch? "Being totally honest, I bloody loved it. Me and the kids had a lovely evening just us three watching films and chilling, and then I got the bed to myself, it was heaven. I think to be honest it was too soon to be missing him, and I've had today on my mind. We've been texting and talking though he seems fine just worried I am going to end things, I think. I said I would see him tomorrow; I think he's taking me out for some food and a few drinks which will be nice as we've not done that for ages." I took a sip of my drink, choked and spat it all over someone walking past to their seat, "fuck, I'm so sorry". Needless to say, the individual wasn't impressed, they just gave me a dirty look, huffed and walked off. Lisa was absolutely pissing herself, and once I'd stopped feeling so mortified so did I.

For pretty much the entire journey we had a little party on the train, I had my Spotify playing random cheesy hits on my phone and we had a little dancing and singing session. Thankfully there was hardly anyone else on the train, and most found it entertaining, although we were asked to keep it down once by the woman I spat my champagne on. After the first time of asking she gave up and proceeded to give us death glares for most of the way. I thought we were very entertaining and in fact everyone on the train should've paid for the entertainment we provided them with.

By the time we'd reached London, as predicted I was very fucking drunk, and as I stepped off the train fell flat on my face, in front of around 1000 people. Great, I would never be classy. If that would've happened back home people would've laughed, then helped you up and made sure you were ok. Not here, oh no, even Lisa fucking left me there, in all fairness she didn't know I'd fallen until she turned to talk to me and had noticed I'd disappeared. We had to walk cross legged out of the train station because we were laughing so much, we were trying not to piss ourselves; we must've looked a right picture. I bet security had a wonderful time watching our escapades on the CCTV, knowing us we'd end up on 'You've Been Framed' or something.

"Right where now?" like she even had to ask. "First things first we need a pub, so we can eat, and I need a piss before I make a mess everywhere." People really didn't like me around here, or the vile manner of which I spoke, this was evident by the stinking looks I was getting thrown my way. I had to stop drinking; it really did bring out the twat in me, more so than usual.

We found a nearby pub, which was full of people dressed up for the Comicon and they looked amazing, some people must've spent thousands on costumes, it was crazy to see. I felt really underdressed now in comparison to everyone else, in my jeans, low cut top and biker jacket. I'd never been to one of these before so didn't really know what the vibe was. Hopefully there will be others there that aren't dressed up like me, or I was really going to look out of place.

After we'd eaten the biggest, fattest, juiciest burgers ever, sobered up a little bit we headed to Oxford Street for some retail therapy, although we couldn't buy a lot because we would have to carry it around with us all day. I'd managed to get some lovely gifts for the kids though and some nice gift sets from one of my favourite shops, Lush.

Once we'd walked our legs off, we decided to make our way to the event. Now I was getting nervous, this place was busier than a brothel on a free hand job night! I had an hour to wait before I had to get into the queue for the meet and greet, and the sights were just something else. There was everything from Thor to Vampires to Obi Wan and furry's, which I had never heard of but they were fantastic. We had selfies with nearly everyone as we were waiting and had some interesting conversations.

We were having so much fun I lost track of time, "Sophie, you need to leave to go queue up to meet Finn." My god I felt sick, I couldn't believe I was actually doing this, but I had nothing to lose, I guess. "Good luck Soph, it'll all be fine, don't stress ok, just be cool and try not to explode when you talk to him." With that, I power walked through the reception. This place was so big, I had no clue where the hell I was going, so I just followed everyone else. Then I came to two big double doors with a sign saying 'Finn Holston – meet and greet, VIP ticket holders only'. Oh, my fucking fuck, shit just got real, I had to take a deep breath and compose myself, I felt a panic attack coming on.

Once I'd calmed myself down a little bit I went through security and then through another set of doors. As I looked up, I could see him, I was at the back of the line, which I guess was a good thing, maybe I would get a little more time because I was last. The line was around fifty people deep, there was a desk at the end of the room, where he was doing autographs and then a Perspex screen so he could stand one side and we could stand the other side to have pictures. Well, it was clear I had a bit of a wait in store, which was good as I could practice what I was going to say again, in my head of course. Then the fucker in front of me kept making conversation with me and I couldn't focus. I politely nodded and smiled and agreed with whatever they were saying, but to be honest I had zoned out and had no idea what they were fucking on about.

Then I looked over towards Finn and he stared straight at me, we both paused, stunned for a moment before he gave me the most amazing smile and wink, I think I came right there on the spot. I had to look away quickly as I blushed, I never fucking blush. At least he didn't look angry that I was here or worried, and he hadn't legged it out of the door yet shouting "Stalker!" For the next thirty minutes I queued, and Finn continued to look over, but I couldn't meet his gaze, so I would have a sneaky look when he wasn't looking. I couldn't even explain the way I was feeling right now, I was panicking, nervous, excited, and I could feel the adrenaline rushing through my veins, and the suspense was killing me.

Chapter 16

Meeting Finn, again

As I got closer to him, he didn't take his eyes off me, that's how it felt anyway, he seemed to be rushing through everyone to get to me. I thought it was me imagining things until the man in front said, "He's not spending much time with everyone, it's as if he just wants this over and done with so he can go home, which is a bit rude. When we came and met Chris Evans, he spent at least five minutes with each person." This just solidified what I thought, maybe he just wanted to get seeing me out of the way, who bloody knows what was going through his head! "Yes, well he is probably a right arrogant knob then." As I said that the room went quiet, I giggled to myself as I said it, and then fucking regretted it later. Everyone looked at me and Finn didn't look too pleased, right I had to behave myself now.

As the man in front of me got his turn with Finn, I was starting to really shit my pants now. His eyes felt like they we're burning a hole in my skull and I couldn't even look at him; I was trying not to giggle nervously and look mentally unstable. Fuck it was my turn, OH MY GOD!

"Sophie? I thought that was you, I am so pleased to see you again you wouldn't believe." Well, I wasn't expecting that, he really was a fucking lying bastard. "I'm here for one reason and one reason only." I began really sternly until I looked into his eyes and I felt that electricity between us, the chemistry I felt with him was unlike nothing I had ever experienced before. My stomach and vagina were betraying me and making me feel like I couldn't say anything more. I just wanted to grab hold of him and feel his tongue all over mine again, my thoughts were fucking racing like fuck. "And why's that?" he reminded me I hadn't finished my sentence, knob. "I want closure on that weekend in Amsterdam, you fucking ghosted me, you prick." With that, he moved the Perspex from between us, and said "It's ok, I know her" to the security guards. He grabbed my arms, and I felt a huge surge of electricity flow through my veins, so much so I inhaled deeply with shock. "Sophie, it's really not what you think at all. You gave me the wrong fucking phone number; I've been going stir crazy knowing you probably thought I had stood you up." Oh, fuck that makes sense, I always gave the wrong number out to guys I didn't like, and very often gave it out by mistake when there was one I actually liked since it didn't happen very often. This still didn't explain why he stood me up though, he could've showed up and met me as we'd arranged. "As for us meeting up" Christ was he psychic? "I was filming Saturday morning, then the producers changed location and we had to go to Germany. I went to the bar lunchtime in the hope you may have been there, and I had no way to call you. I had to leave, and I've regretted it ever since. I really didn't ghost you; I couldn't wait to see you." Well fuck I was not expecting that. I just stood in a state of shock looking up at his amazing face, and with that he slid his hand through my hair onto the back of my neck and pulled me into him for a kiss, I didn't want it to end and then I remembered Caleb and pulled away. Fuck what had I got myself into?

"I'm sorry Sophie, do you forgive me? I really want to see you properly, but I have to go and give an interview now to all of the fans. Can I have your proper number this time so we can meet up when I get off?" He looked at me with those beautiful blue eyes and I was lost again; I would do anything for this man, he was simply beautiful. "Give me your number this time and I will message you now so there is no confusion. As for meeting up, what time? Me and my mate have to get back home, we have a train booked." He put his number in my phone and I messaged him there and then to make sure, and sure enough his phone went off, and he smiled from ear to ear. "There we go that wasn't so hard was it, you're never getting rid of me now Miss Rush, I have your number." Fucking loved the sound of that, so much so my heart skipped a beat, I didn't want to get rid of him, I hadn't stopped thinking about him for weeks. "I don't get off until five, what time is your train?" Fuck, well this was shit. "My train is at 4:30, so that's that idea out of the window. I don't think Lisa would be too pleased if I made her late, she has to be back and so do I really." I actually wanted to stay with him and never go home, but that was just unrealistic. "That's ok I understand, I really want to see you properly, I'll come to Wales if I need to." Then security piped up "Mr Holston, we really need to leave now, you're already late." Oh, fuck off, don't take him away from me not yet. "Yes, yes, I know I'm coming now just two more seconds! Sophie, I have to go but I'll message you when I'm done, and we can chat on the phone and sort something out where we can see each other properly. I really like you, and you're all I could think about for the last few weeks." This time I pulled his head down to mine and kissed him like I was never going to see him again. I really fucking wanted him, and he could feel how much. We pulled away and he said "Fuck, Sophie what are you doing to me? Have a safe trip back, I am so fucking happy I saw you again." And with that he was whisked out of the room and I stood there shell shocked. What the fuck had just happened?

Once I'd recovered from the shock a little bit, I went to find Lisa, bless her she'd been on her own for about an hour, hope she hadn't been stuck with some fucking weirdo chewing her ear off the whole time. It took me another 10 minutes, but I found her eventually, and sure enough she was sitting there looking fed up with someone talking her head off. She saw me and I'd never seen her looking so relieved in all her life, god knows how long she'd been stuck there. "Lisa, come on we're going to miss the train." Thought I'd save her and also selfishly myself, rather than getting stuck there talking myself. I never saw her move so fast; she was like a cheetah on speed. "It was lovely to meet you, take care of yourself, am really sorry but I have to leave now." I heard her say to the guy "Oh that's a shame, was lovely to meet you beautiful." And with that he took her hand and kissed it, she just looked utterly disgusted, and I couldn't stop pissing myself, like the good friend I was.

"Ha ha, that was brilliant, who's the fella Lisa?" And with that she nudged me, and I went flying across the room and hit a sign over. Everyone saw and made a 'ooooo' noise. "Fucking cheers Lisa, me falling over once today wasn't enough for you was it? She helped me up. "Enough of that shit, what the fuck happened in there, you were gone for eternity. I want to know every last fucking detail; did you get the closure you needed to move on?" Christ, where was I going to start? "Well, I got answers, but no I can't move on. I gave him the wrong phone number and he had to leave for Germany before he could see me, he grabbed me and kissed me and we exchanged numbers. Then I remembered I am in a relationship with Caleb, what have I done? Finn asked me to meet up with him tonight, but I said we had to get back. Basically, we left it that we would meet up, I think he is going to potentially come to Wales to see me. Now my head is even more fucked, but honestly, I feel really happy, it wasn't all in my head and I wasn't going crazy all this time, the feeling was mutual." Lisa went quiet as she processed the information for a second or two, then she made me jump when she screamed "Oh my fucking god Sophie! I am so happy for you, I hoped this would happen, but when you were gone for so long, I expected the worst. What are you going to do?" This was the one question I didn't have an answer to. "Honestly, I have no clue, Finn doesn't know about Caleb and vice versa, I have to figure this out and I need to do it quickly."

Chapter 17

What the fuck am I going to do?

Fuck, we ran like fuck to get the train, I was so unfit it was unreal, my tits didn't help matters they were swinging all over the place, I really shouldn't run without a sports bra on. As we got comfy in our seats and I caught my breath I checked my phone. There were two messages, one from Caleb and one from Finn. I told Lisa and she said "Right this is putting it really simply for you, maybe too simple, but which one do you want to read first? Which are you most happy about getting?" Well, that was obvious "Finn of course, but is that because he is every girl's dream? And me and Caleb have been arguing constantly. This is a total fucking mess, what am I going to do? I'm meant to be seeing Caleb tomorrow and I can't go like this; I need to sort my head out." Just as I was about to read Finn's message he'd messaged again, he was rather impatient to say the least, normally this would piss me off, but I fucking loved it from him. The first message read 'I'm so glad I saw you today, I've felt totally shit ever since that weekend, I thought I'd never see you again'. Then, he followed it up with 'can we Facetime when you get home?' He definitely sounded like he couldn't wait to speak to me again, and I felt the same, but I also felt guilty, at the end of the day I was in a relationship with another man.

After hours of using Lisa as a counsellor on the way home and messaging both Caleb and Finn, I was ready to get back home where I could start figuring out what the fucking hell I was going to do. I think I had bored Lisa half to death as she was fast asleep, I had to wake her up once we'd arrived back at the train station. "Come on lazy bitch get up, we're home, well we will be once we get in your car and you drive us there." She looked shattered; to be fair it had been a very long day. I knew there would be no sleeping for me tonight though, I was too excited and burdened with what I should do.

I finally got in and gave the kids the biggest hug ever, I just needed to hold my children right now and not think of anything else. They didn't know anything about Finn, they didn't know I'd met him in Amsterdam or anything, I know what their take on it would be; pick Finn, he's loaded and famous and they thought that would make them famous and loaded. We put a film on, it was Marie's turn to pick, and be it coincidence or not she picked one of Finn's films. I was most definitely not going to complain, I couldn't believe this man actually wanted me back. I'd felt lust before, but this was another level and I could understand that I wanted him, what I couldn't wrap my head around was the fact he wanted me back. I wasn't like the women he had contact with on a daily basis. I didn't look like a supermodel, I was chunky and looked nothing like the women he could've had. But you couldn't make that chemistry up, it was another level, but was it sustainable? Did he just want 'a bit a rough' and after he's had his fun, he'd meet someone on set, cheat on me and leave me and I'd be fucking heartbroken and look like a fool.

Then there was Caleb. I loved him yes, but, it wasn't what I'd imagined it would be; there was something missing from the moment we got together and a part of me wondered if it would've been missing if I had never met Finn. Before Finn had come along, I'd wanted Caleb for such a long time and now I felt as if I was lying to myself. What we had was no fairy tale, and I was fully aware life wasn't meant to be that way, but I wasn't happy either and surely if Caleb was the one I wouldn't want someone else, I wouldn't be fantasizing about Finn when Caleb fucked me.

I knew in my heart what I wanted to do and what was the best thing for me, it just wouldn't be easy. I had to see both of them face to face, first would be Caleb, I'll invite him over tomorrow so we can sit down and chat rather than go out and speak in public, then I'll speak to Finn once I've sorted things with Caleb.

That night I went to bed and dreamt about this whole clusterfuck, I tossed and turned all night, going over a million different scenarios in my head. So, by the time morning came I looked as rough as a badger's ass! But I dragged myself up, showered and put my face on ready to face Caleb and tell him the truth. I couldn't eat breakfast because I felt sick to my stomach. As I waited for Caleb, I reflected on everything we had been through. I did love him, he was amazing person, and we had a good thing going before this fucking pandemic. Then there was a knock at the door, I got my ass up and braced myself before I unlocked it.

As I looked through the glass on my door, I saw two figures outside. That was odd, who else was there? I didn't have to wait long to find out. As I opened the door Caleb and Finn were both standing there, looking confused. Caleb glared at me and said,

"What the fuck is going on Sophie?"

To be continued…….

Dedication

I want to thank all of my wonderful family and friends for all the love and support they have provided over the last few months, in particular my brother and sister Jason and Stacey and close friends Paul, Natalie and Mel. I know this is pretty much all I have spoken about for the last few months.

To my fabulous sister-in-law Emma, for being my guinea pig and doing a fantastic job of editing the book for me.

To my wonderful mother Lilian, I hope you don't read this book ha, ha but will be proud of me anyway.

To my father Alfie, my hero, I miss you every day and I hope I always make you proud.

To my children, Nicole and Naomi, you are my world, reach for the star's girls, you can achieve anything you want to.

Last but not least, thank you to you, the readers for spurring me on and enjoying my work.

Printed in Great Britain
by Amazon

75098542R00135